The Wandora Unit

by

Jessy Randall

Ghost Road Press

Denver, CO

Ghost Road Press

820 S. Monaco Pkwy #288

Denver, CO 80024

www.ghostroadpress.com

Interior Design: Evan Lee and Matt Davis
The Wandora Unit
Ghost Road Press
ISBN 978-0-9816525-8-0; 0-9816525-8-1
Library of Congress Control Number: 2009927143

ACKNOWLEDGMENTS

Almost all the poems in *The Wandora Unit* are by high school students. Unless otherwise specified, the poems first appeared in *Galaxy*, the literary magazine of Brighton High School in Rochester, New York. The author gratefully acknowledges Anna Bendiksen ("You went…"), Suzanne M. DeGrasse ("Loom"), Valerie Douglas ("Ode to School," originally published as "Ode to Africa"), H.K. ("No More to Abide in the Garden"), Ishmael Klein ("To Jar," first printed in *Upstart*, a literary magazine at Columbia University), Liz Lowe ("Tanglewood"), Robin Nelson ("In dreams…"), Daniel M. Shapiro ("I see you…"), Amy Shuffelton ("Blueberries" and "Jungle"), and Judy Wolf ("Thank You," "Out onto the morning…," and the unpublished "One Brief Moment"). "School: A Start in Life" was printed anonymously. The "I hated camp" paragraph in the section beginning "Okay, Galaxians, on to the next…" is from Ethan Borg's short story "The Roar it Preached," first printed in *Galaxy* and used by permission of the author. "A Walk on Monroe Avenue" is a modified version of an unpublished poem told to the author by Josh Newman, who heard it from Adam Hurwich, who heard it from a classmate whose name is lost to the ravages of time. All other poems are by Jessy Randall. "A Poem" and "Click" first appeared in *Galaxy*; "Cheshire Poem" first appeared in the online chapbook *Dorothy Surrenders*; "The incompleteness…" first appeared in *Explosive Magazine*; "After School" first appeared (in slightly different form) in the chapbook *Broken Heart Diet*; and "Romance Novels" first appeared in *Drunken Boat*.

For Amy

PART I

People have always told me I have a strong personality. I'm never sure if it's a compliment. Now that I'm friends with Wanda, people say *we* have a strong personality. We don't care whether it's a compliment or not – it's definitely true.

Wanda and I live across the street from each other and walk to school together every day. School starts at 7:15 in the morning, because of some insane administrator's idea of efficient scheduling. After school Wanda has orchestra practice and I have play rehearsal, so we walk home at different times.

At 7:15 in the morning Wanda and I have gym. That means we play soccer in the dark. We can barely tell who is on the blue pinney team and who is on the red. We try to avoid gym. Sometimes we can get our periods for three weeks out of four! (Mr. Summers is too embarrassed to say anything.) When we "have our periods," we sit on the bleachers making up schemes to improve Galaxy.

The promise in those words! Some schools (as Ms. Green, the magazine advisor, constantly reminds us) don't even *have* a literary magazine, much less a room to hang around in. (Ms. Green is my favorite teacher in the whole school. She does not ever come in the Galaxy room. She knows that if she did, she'd have to tell the principal about the paper towels, what's written on the walls, and Kapcki Mapcki.)

This is the second year that Wanda and I are editing Galaxy, and due to our aggressive junior year campaign, it is now a real publication, almost as real as the newspaper or the yearbook, and it even has its own office, albeit small and windowless. The members of Galaxy (and anyone else who knows about it and is interested) can go in the room on their free mods. This is a great relief, of course, because of the frightening nature of the cafeteria, where most kids go. The Galaxy room – when it is open, when Wanda and I unlock it – is a safe haven, a place where you can do exactly what you want to, which is usually just sit around.

Right now eleven people are in the Galaxy room playing Kapcki Mapcki, a game involving (among other things, this time around) a metal pole found in the school dumpster, a bookshelf, two wastebaskets, and a line of masking tape on the floor. When a piece of paper flies through the air and a pen cap hits the ceiling, one kid dives under the typewriter table yelling "tie game." My best friends are here and also some really annoying people and some new people who think everyone here is weird.

It is better to be weird than to be boring. At our school sometimes that is the choice.

§   §   §

```
Kill all cliche's
```
types Wanda's boyfriend Norris on the scroll.

Galaxy members steal rolls of paper towel from the boys' bathroom down the hall and stick them in the manual typewriter, which has no correction tape and no backspace key. Anyone can type anything on the scroll, and when it gets about eight feet of typing on it someone will attach it to the wall with masking tape.

```
Why do peoplye fall in love/?
     Becasuse they are stiupid
     Because they need a date to the prom
     You gusys are both wrogn people fall in
lvoe to find out each other's faults. Once each
person has foudn out all the other person'sf
faults they breack up and fall in love with
someone new to findout new faults.
     That's  the  sickest  thing  I:Ve  ever
heard.
     Oh  yeah  you  think  tha'ts  sick  well
fdfmxhey! Youw ca'tn
     Yes I can mwahwhwahaha
```

§   §   §

"I have your book," I say to Wanda as soon as she answers the phone.

"And I have your book."

"Shall we trade?"

"I'll see you in thirty seconds." Wanda's family has about eight million books. Both her parents are professors. Some day, when I have my own place, I am going to have tons of books the way they do, spilling out of bookshelves in every room. Wanda is glad to lend me books, and I often borrow stuff at the library for her.

We meet in the road mid-way between our houses. We stand there talking, barefoot, the pavement still warm from the afternoon sun. When a car comes, we glide to the left or the right, returning each time to the road's center. After five or ten minutes, we start to walk slowly back to our separate houses, still facing each other, still talking, louder and louder as we get further away from each other until the final yell: "See you tomorrow!" "See you..."

§　§　§

A lot of Galaxy submissions are depressed love poems. Wanda and I agree that a depressed love poem is like a picture of a shoe. Occasionally it can be done really well but it's still just a shoe. Some people who hang around in the Galaxy room don't write at all, but they like to read poetry or they just like the idea of Galaxy. Or they have no place to sit in the cafeteria, so they spend mod 13 in the Galaxy room and get sucked into the weirdness and start going there on all their free mods to type on the scroll or participate in the Kapcki Mapcki games or (in at least one case) just to sit in a chair and do nothing. Some of the poets of the school don't ever come to Galaxy meetings, and that is fine too.

§　§　§

Wanda and I: brown-haired, medium-size, semi-pretty. We do not mind being mistaken for each other.

When I got the lead in the musical, people congratulated Wanda. When Wanda was voted president of the Model United Nations, people begged me to be made country heads. Wanda and I like the confusion. We think it is fun.

§   §   §

Chapter XXVI: In Which Wanda and I, On Our Way to School at 7:03 a.m., Discuss the Afterlife:

Walking with Wanda on the way to school, I say that in heaven I would never have to walk. I would just wish to be somewhere and then be there. I am grouchy from staying up too late talking to my boyfriend Ernie on the phone. (Even though we've been going out for a year, it still gives me a thrill to say that: "my boyfriend, Ernie." I have a boyfriend! He is tall, with curly red hair. He always calls me at ten and says loopy, lovey things that make no sense.)

Anyhow, Wanda says her heaven would be an infinite picnic by a lake with all her friends. I immediately want to change what I said about the afterlife, and switch to her answer. That happens a lot when we talk – we start out with our own opinions, and sort of meld them together, one way or the other or a combination. It is like we collaborate on our thoughts until we come up with THE thoughts. The thoughts for us.

By the time we get to school Wanda and I have invited all the guests to the afterlife picnic, chosen a menu, and decided on the weather. I am wearing Josh's wristwatch. All is right with the world.

§ § §

The height chart in the Galaxy room is written directly on the wall in black marker. It starts with Yoda at three feet three inches and ends with Manute Bol at twelve feet. Wanda and I are five feet four inches tall. Norris is five feet eight inches; Simon on the shoulders of Josh is ten feet three and one half inches; Norris's ego is "The size of Los Angeles"; Ray's penis is three feet four inches (one inch higher than Yoda); Ernie's aura (according to arrows) covers the whole room.

Ernie is typing on the scroll right now:

```
BUFF   JOHNSON's   masculene   muscalure   chest
expands to break the wempy ropes that bend him,
but  su ddenly  hes  worst  nightsmare  arrives.
THe Wandora Unet throws open the door to the
dungeon and takes a .45 from the holstere
slung aroudn ets shared hip.  'That's et for
you BUff you'll nevere say the word retard
again'
```

"Well, you shouldn't say that word, Ernie."

"Just because we ganged up on you about it doesn't mean we're wrong."

"You can quit all that ferocious typing, Ernie, and just admit that we're right."

"Yeah, you should just face it."

"And what is that 'Wandora Unit' thing? What is that? Are you trying to say that we're, like, attached at the hip or something?"

"All I'm saying is, you look alike, you dress alike, and you are always together. It seems like you can't go anywhere without each other. You can't even have opinions without each other. That's what I mean." Ernie gets a little red in the face, not because he doesn't believe what he is saying, but because he has never said it out loud before.

"You just wish you had a best friend."

"Yeah, you just wish you were friends with someone like we're friends."

"In fact, you're wrong. You two are just wrong. I know you don't think you can ever be wrong but in this case you are. I don't wish that at all! I am too, um, individualistic to want your kind of friendship."

"That's it, we're making a rule: no boyfriends in the Galaxy room."

"Yeah, Ernie, go away, I'll meet you at your locker later, okay?"

"Why should I leave? I have as much right to be here as you."

Wanda and I look at each other and laugh. We are the *editors*. We can do whatever we want, and no one can stop us.

§   §   §

Here is one of the index cards someone put on the Galaxy room door:

Divide writers into two main categories:

A. Those who write with a sense of responsibility to the life of the mind.

B. Those who do without it.

– Ezra Pound, *The ABC of Writing*

§ § §

It's a well-known fact that the library is going to be renovated next year and the Galaxy room is going to be blown up. That's why we feel free to draw on the walls; that's why nobody stopped Norris from painting above the typewriter, in huge pink letters, "I sound my barbaric YAWP over the roofs of the world." That's why, somehow, when Spandau Ballet's "This Much Is True" plays on the radio, and Ernie kisses me, it feels like it counts double, and at the same time it feels like it doesn't count at all. Because soon the place where we are won't even exist.

Galaxy members seldom go to the cafeteria except to buy donuts and stuff. If you eat the school food you have to deal with the "a la carte" lunch lady, so named because she repeats that phrase over and over each day as the lunch line slogs its way past her. "A la carte? You're welcome. Next? A la carte?"

The cafeteria is full of horrible tables with round chairs attached, like plastic centipedes all around the low-ceilinged room, and you have to know which table is yours. God forbid you sit at the wrong table. If you did everyone would probably get up and move and soon the cafeteria would be a screaming riot. Galaxy members do not have a table of their own so the Galaxy room becomes our cafeteria table. We are freaks, poetic freaks, but at least we have a place to go, so we go there, always, every chance we get on our school's bizarre modular system.

Each mod is eighteen minutes long; most classes are three mods, fifty-four minutes. We get five minutes between classes, which is not enough time to get from AP Physics in the basement to AP English on the fourth floor at the other end of the building as I have to do four days out of six. (The schedule works on a six day cycle, so we have Day 1, Day 2, etcetera, and you don't have to miss Monday and Friday classes on long weekends because the cycle just wraps around. I don't know of any other school that does things this way.)

The benefit of the system is that you get free mods sometimes. You are supposed to go to a media center (the foreign language center, the math science center, the extra help center) on your free mods but they are free and no one forces you to go to a center, unless you are a freshman, in which case you have a yellow card you have to get stamped. Mrs. Finkle, the librarian, is in charge of stamping the yellow cards; she strikes terror into the hearts of freshmen.

Occasionally Galaxy members do venture into the cafeteria to solicit poems or to gather more Galaxy members or to try to earn money to pay the printer. Other clubs sell flower-grams, balloon-o-grams, candy-grams – we sell sock-o-grams, but this has not proven very lucrative. Next we try having a Crantastic stand, and Galaxy members volunteer to do a dramatic reading of the conversation printed on the back of the container: "This is crantastic!" "Don't you mean fantastic?" "No, Crantastic™...", but we barely break even.

Ray suggests the Galaxy members sell our souls but much arguing ensues about whether or not there is such a thing as a soul, and if there is, how much should it cost? Ray then suggests we sell our bodies, but no one goes along with this. Finally, Galaxy has a used book sale which is quite a success, especially since (we find out later) Simon does some under-the-table business (he literally sits under the table) selling his father's old *Playboy*s.

§ § §

While I hand out copies of this week's poems, Wanda stands in the middle of Simon's living room making announcements. "The last line of #7, 'The Swamp of Love,' should read 'Your disease is in my mouth,' and not 'Your disease is in my mouse.' We apologize for the typing error. Let us now turn to poem #6, the one that begins 'A poem is not for throwing.'"

"That one was funny."

"Good obnoxiousness."

"I don't get it."

"I think it's supposed to be ironical."

"Ironical? Don't you mean *ironic*?"

"Look it up, ironical is a totally acceptable word."

"You just want to have an extra syllable on there. I bet you say *partially*, too. And *utilize*."

"Back to the poem, please."

"Well, it's not about suicide at least."

§   §   §

This is the way Wanda and I met. When we were in seventh grade, we were the only girls in the Challenge Program, except for Laurie Leach who was extremely skinny and who got voted Girl Most Likely to Succeed every year. We did not like Laurie Leach and her monogrammed sweaters, but we didn't really like each other, either; we didn't like girls our own age in general since we had both suffered the kind of cruelty only pre-adolescent girls can inflict: "We have a secret we can't tell you" "Vickie is my best friend now instead of you" "We think you dress slutty" "We only invited you because we feel sorry for you, but we'll try to help you change."

The Challenge assignment one week was to make a box that would heat up ten degrees in ten minutes in the sun. Mrs. Erwin said "Please work in groups of two," and I wanted to be partners with Kenny Morris, who was really cute but never washed his hair. At the age of twelve, I did not have the nerve to introduce myself to Kenny, but since he talked too much, even more than I did, no one else picked him. No one picked me either and I looked down at the floor until the bell rang.

It turned out that no one picked anyone ("Don't you think those Challenge Program kids are a bit too, well, independent?" the school principal once asked Mrs. Erwin, causing smoke to come out of her ears) and so we had to be assigned partners randomly. Kenny Morris got Laurie Leach, which was so unfair, because Laurie didn't even like him! But Wanda and I got each other. Sometimes I wonder if Mrs. Erwin put us together on purpose, in which case I should send her a nine-page thank-you letter.

None of the boxes heated up more than three degrees in twenty minutes anyway, no matter how much tinfoil anyone used, so Mrs. Erwin made a curriculum adjustment from creative science to creative logic. No one had to have a partner and everyone was happy, each kid spending the full three mods drawing a matrix and carefully filling it in. But from then on Wanda and I walked to school together.

§   §   §

Ray wins the annual Kapcki Mapcki tournament by inventing a rule during the finals so ingenious that only he can follow it. It has something to do with higher math.

He wins the prize, which is six boxes of lime Jell-O mix.

§   §   §

"Well, I think we've pretty much talked #11 into the ground. Anyone want to start the discussion of #12, 'School: A Start in Life'?"

"Gross."

"But school does destroy us, right?"

"Only if we let it."

"But it does try. You know I read somewhere that

the main purpose of school is not to educate us..."

"But to socialize us?"

"Not even that. To babysit us. So our parents can work."

"So it's all because of the capitalist pigs!"

"Kapcki Mapcki to the rescue!"

"We are not playing Kapcki Mapcki in Melissa's living room."

"No, I just meant..."

"I agree totally with this poem. Supposedly we go to school to learn things and digest things but instead we just turn into part of the school."

"Or into each other."

§   §   §

When we drive home from trips, we know we are almost there when we see the Wegmans trucks, white with red letters, on the highway. We sigh with glee. Soon we are able to pick up Rochester radio stations. When we see each other again we stay up late telling all the things we did on our vacations, and at two in the morning we go to Wegmans for no real reason, just to go. We look forward to seeing Marvin Marsh there with his Wegmans uniform shirt buttoned all the way to the top. Simon always sees someone he knows at Wegmans and we all have to wait around until he finishes talking. We buy practically nothing: batteries, or pens, or a can of Pringles.

Wegmans is a gigantic grocery store with videos and lawn chairs and its own bank machine and a place to develop your film and aisles and aisles of food. The aisles are wider than normal, wider than needed. It's open all night with a gate made of grocery carts and it's better than Tops, better than Star, better than Super Duper. You could easily live there for weeks and have a very happy life. Wegmans is part of our collective unconscious. We dream about it, strange dreams in which it grows huge and maze-like.

The Cobb's Hill reservoir also recurs in our dreams. A ten-minute walk from our neighborhood, the reservoir is at the top of a tree-studded hill so that when you are at the top you can see the high, middle, and elementary schools and, in the other direction, the dull Rochester skyline. At the bottom of the hill are tennis courts and a playground and a pond for ice-skating. Cobb's Hill is a center: for Brighton kids, it is where everything outdoors happens. We jog and sled and take picnics there; it is the place where Simon and Josh got lost and became friends before they got to be friends with Wanda and me, which happened in eighth grade when they pretended to play football right in our front yards as if they didn't know we lived there.

§   §   §

Each friend represents a world in us, a world possibly not born until they arrive, and it is only by this meeting that a new world is born.

– Anais Nin

§ § §

After Galaxy meeting, the five of us – Josh, Simon, Ray, Wanda, and I – squash into a booth at the Highland Park Diner.

"My favorite moment," says Ray, "Was when you" (he points with his chin at Simon) "said Yvonne was being obtuse, and she got all insulted and said her weight had nothing to do with it."

"Why is Galaxy attracting so many dorks this year?" I ask, transporting a strawful of Ray's vanilla milkshake into my coke.

"It could be," says Josh, "that we're just expanding – the group is getting bigger and that means taking on some dorks."

"No, I think literary magazines are always partly populated by idiots," says Wanda. "There are the people who really care, like us, and then there are all these people who just think it's cool to like poetry, but they don't actually like poetry at all."

A long, five-way conversation ensues on the use of clichés. The discussion then moves on to the true definition of nerdiness, and whether smart people can ever be anything other than nerds.

Whoever's talking at the time, everyone looks at that person, the eyes moving from Simon to Josh to me to Ray to me to Josh to Wanda to me to Wanda to Ray…

§ § §

Soon after Wanda and I started walking to school together, Kenny Morris washed his hair and took Laurie Leach to the seventh grade dance. By that time I had a crush on Steve Chin and I didn't have the right kind of dress to wear anyway. Laurie Leach wore a monogrammed strapless and I stayed home and watched a video of *The Dark Crystal* with Steve Chin and his brother whom he had to babysit that night or, he says, he would have asked me to the dance; he was going to ask me, he said, but then he didn't.

The way Steve Chin held my hand that night has never been repeated; it was one of the sexiest hours of my life and I was only thirteen at the time although I felt at least fifteen, maybe even sixteen. I remember trying to explain to Wanda the wonder of Steve Chin's hand-holding, but it was impossible, and then Steve Chin moved to Ohio and I found out that Wanda had been keeping a journal just like I had, for five years both of us had been keeping journals full of poems that no one ever saw. And that is how we started being friends.

§   §   §

```
are Wanda and dora teh same person?
they wish They were.
If Wadna and Dora were the same person, they
would be the president.
They already thenk they own the world.
I don't want the world, I just want yoru
half.
```

Does anyoen e knwo whothat kid is who comes in
here and jsut sits ina chair and doesn't talk
to anyone?
Maybe he is a brilliant poet.
Maybe he is a total moron.
His name is Bill Brunheuber.
From now on sitting in a chair and not talkign
should be called brunheuberring.
Hey that's mean.
nice=boring   brunheubering=boring
boring=boring
there fore Bill Breunhueber is a nice guy and
we should all try to be freends with him.
That was a really good Proof.
I dont want to be 'Freends' wuth anyone maybe
friends or freinds but not 'freends'.

§   §   §

No matter where Ernie is in the school, I am aware
of him. I orchestrate chance meetings. Knowing I'll see
him soon, I feel extra alive in class.

Sometimes I think I want to infuse every moment
of my life with drama, for every moment to be full of
intense meaning – not the weather, not what anyone ate
for lunch, but important things: love, friendship, passion,
music, literature, art. Perhaps this is why I enjoy a
certain melancholia, or anyway find sadness preferable to
blandness. Small talk makes me want to run from the room
and burst into tears.

The only person who understands this is Wanda. Even as I'm feeling these crazy feelings for Ernie, it's Wanda I want to tell about it. If I can't tell Wanda, I'll write in my notebook. Ms. Green says that poetry lets you have your feelings instead of your feelings having you. I write, hoping the truth about my life will rise to the top like marshmallows in hot chocolate powder when you shake the container.

§   §   §

Ernie speaks:

I don't really have a theory about Dora and Wanda's friendship, but I've always wondered if maybe they had the hots for each other, you know? Even for just one time, like, an experiment. Anyway, I'm probably the only one who knows why they stopped being friends at the end of high school, or stopped being the Wandora Unit, anyway. It's because when Dora and I broke up, Dora was really upset. Crying all the time and staying home from school and not talking to people. She pissed Wanda off by being so depressed, and Wanda got fed up and walked out on her. Who can blame Wanda though, you know? People like that are a drag.

§ § §

From my journal:

My love is so big
you can not get your arms around it
you can not carry the grand piano of my love
up the stairs
I present you
with a refrigerator box of love, a meadow
of it and who can lift a meadow, a planet,
a cliff extending in all directions

So I'll shrink it, I'll shrink it, I am
shrinking it even as I write. Soon my love
for you will be so tiny it will be like
the princess's pea and I won't be able
to feel it through all those mattresses

§ § §

For Wanda and me, this entire past month has been taken up with a great book called *The Mists of Avalon*.

I get it at the library, carrying it home on my bike – it's 876 pages long and weighs a ton under my arm and gives me a bruise, and I almost crash trying to steer one handed. But the pain is totally worth it because I have never read a book like this. It's about the knights of the round table, but you can hardly recognize the stories. Morgan le Fay is the main character, and she's not a bad witch at all, but a good witch, like Glinda.

When I am halfway through it, I press the book upon Wanda (it is the only copy the Brighton Public Library owns), and it is all we talk about in the morning on the way to school.

The book takes us a full month to read, because we pass it back and forth like salt at the dinner table. We leave it in the Galaxy room during the day, and each read it on our free mods. Norris and Ernie are shushed if they try to talk to us. The book is so *good*; it seems to be the truest version of the stories; everything in it makes *sense*.

We quote Morgan le Fay in our classes. We understand all other books in relation to this book. Soon we begin to think of our own lives in its terms. We both want to be Morgana: misunderstood, powerful, wise, able to cast spells. Suddenly the legend of King Arthur belongs to us, as if we wrote the myths ourselves. I have to ride back to the library twice to renew the book.

We read the last fifty pages together, lying on Wanda's living room floor on a Sunday afternoon, turning the pages after glancing at each other to be sure we're ready. We laugh helplessly at how our noses are running, how the tears are falling onto the pages. But neither of us can leave the book to get a tissue.

§   §   §

"I think #16 is about nuclear war."
"Depression, disaster...a broken heart?"
"All I know is," says Yvonne Pie, an insipid girl

with half her head shaved, "is I don't like it."

I ask her, as patiently as possible, "What don't you like about it, Yvonne?"

"I don't know. I can't explain. I just don't like it."

Wanda explains, "But that is not a useful comment. What do you think the poem is *about*? What does it *mean*? That is what we're discussing here. Not our personal opinions on the worth of the poem – there'll be time for that when we vote at the end of the year."

Gina Marcone, from her throne-like position in the only comfortable chair in Josh's living room, Gina, who coincidentally has the opposite half of her head shaved than Yvonne, remarks that personally she likes the poem, really really a lot.

"And what do you like about it?

Gina is as incapable of articulating a response as Yvonne, and just giggles helplessly. "It's just a good poem, I think."

The discussion returns to explication.

"Nuclear war, or maybe suicide."

"Can we go on to the next please? I'm sick of all this death, it's boring."

§　§　§

Wanda and I find it useful to tell each other our dreams on the way to school. Sometimes, later, we actually forget whose dream was whose, and we each remember the other's dreams as if they were our own.

Wanda's Dream

Dora and I are driving in the car and it is snowing very hard all around. The car lifts up and down. Then we are outside, the car is gone and the snow is paper, many shreds of paper with blue writing on them. It is not cold at all and we try to make snowballs but the paper won't stick and Norris says "These are all your poems, I had them made into a blizzard" and we say thank you. Except Dora is very mad and would have preferred rain.

Dora's Dream

I am in a floating meadow which I know is the moon. It floats about three feet over the normal world but for some reason I can't get down. Some birds explain to me that I am not supposed to be there but they just shrug their shoulders when I ask how to leave. The meadow is very beautiful and I am all alone and then Simon's dad is there in his jogging suit and when I ask him how to get down he says you just have to jog around this track.

"First of all," says Wanda, "You *have* to read this book by Italo Calvino called, um, what's it called, *Cosmicomics*, it's a book of short stories, and there's a story about the moon in there that totally relates. And second of all, Simon's *dad*?

"Yeah, in a jogging suit."

"Does he jog?"

"Not that I know of."

"What color was the jogging suit?"

"Neon green!"

§   §   §

"Who would ever have thought that a good little girl like you could destroy my beautiful wickedness..."

In ninth grade, long before the onset of Ernie and Norris, Josh, Simon, Ray, Wanda, and I watched *The Wizard of Oz* on TV in my basement. Afterward, we flipped the TV off and sat in the dark on the mushy couch spilling our souls.

"So, Dora, who do you like," asked Simon, as soon as we were settled in.

I had no shame and would answer any question, so I told the truth: "Greg Harris" (a forgettable boy, a tenor in the choir at the time, he sang so divinely) and asked Simon in return "And who do you like, it's only fair."

"Ask someone else first."

"Okay, Josh, you never like anyone, who do you like?"

Josh paused, rolled his eyes, and named a drippy skinny blond girl, Crystal Weissman.

"Eww!" Wanda and I were aghast. I suspected he was lying, but did not press him. I had had a funny feeling for a long time that Josh liked me, loved me even. And I was almost right.

Wanda liked a boy in her French class but was too embarrassed to find out his real name. She only knew his French class name, which was Pierre.

Ray liked Rachel Ann Satter, a girl in my English class. I warned him that her poetry was incomprehensible, but he said that all girls (except Wanda and me, who didn't count) were incomprehensible.

Simon, who had started the whole thing, was reluctant to say who he liked, but finally admitted the lucky girl was … Laurie Leach! Everyone else simultaneously pretended to throw up.

§ § §

Gre at Philosophical QUestion of Mod 13:
if you had p ut on a differrent shirt this morning, would you have had a different day?

§ § §

The phenomenon of Country Sweet cannot be explained to people who don't live in Rochester, but I am going to try.

It is a place that sells chicken wings, in the city, open until three in the morning, and Brighton kids go there when they have done everything else there is to do and Perkins has a waiting line. The awning is red; the food is delicious and makes your nose run. Bread is ten cents a slice. With each order you get a handful of wetnaps and you need every one. The Wandora Unit likes our wings mild; Josh and Simon split a dozen mixed. It's a well-known fact that a recent graduate from our school once spent a college weekend driving seventeen hours just for Country Sweet, slept overnight, and then drove seventeen hours back in time for classes on Monday.

Foreign exchange students are periodically taken to Country Sweet where they are politely appalled: "You eat zat?" "I have no hunger, truly, but I thank you." No one who was not an adolescent in Rochester likes the sauce, except perhaps anxious fiancées.

§   §   §

From my journal:

There you are, Wanda, at the movies
with a boyfriend who won't speak
to your other friends. He would rather
sit alone than talk to us.
You are radiant. Your pink face
and wide smile. There you are
going down the aisle. Some day will I be
your maid of honor? And should I ask
why have you become middle aged
when you have nothing to fear?
And where
is the red bathing suit of yesteryear
you wore when we were sixteen on the beach?

this poem sucks.

§ § §

WOrsd and prhrases that describe the Wandrora
Unit:

nice
know-it-alsl
smrart
poetic
pretty
pains in the buttt

words adn phrasees that do not appalply to the
Wanroda Unit:

IN a moment of doubt
shy & demure
Petite
laid bakc
boringg
perky
spotnaneous
sent to Detention
lazy
pre-menstural
unable to find owrds to epxress themselves
skinny
air-heaeded
humble

§ § §

Ernie and I are at a free showing of *Star Wars* in Highland Park. Little kids run around with green light-sticks bought at CVS and cracked open at sunset. The light-sticks swirl on strings and seem not to dim at all. When the kids go home they will put them in the fridge, believing the myth that this will make the light-stick last another night. But the green glow will fade there in the darkness next to the frozen tater tots sometime before morning.

I have brought an old quilt and Ernie and I spread it on the hill. Reaching into the pocket of his windbreaker, Ernie reveals a can of bug spray. The chemical smell of Off! fills the air.

§   §   §

From the orchestra room and out into the crowded hall come Simon and Josh, right at us, walking about twenty feet apart and carrying between them a microphone on a very long cord. Simon, in front, speaks into the microphone: "Hello, Wanda and Dora," and Josh, from behind him, holding the plug of the microphone to his bellybutton, bellows "HELLO WANDA AND DORA." Simon courteously inquires after our health: "And how are you today?" "AND HOW ARE YOU TODAY?" The Wandora Unit is fine. "Oh, good" "OH, GOOD" "And did you know it's cheese fish for lunch" "AND DID YOU KNOW..."

Wanda and I duck into the girls' bathroom to escape this, but what do we discover there? Fifteen popular girls with curling irons, mousse, and hairbrushes! Is nowhere safe? The girls turn from the mirror self-righteously as if to say "This is not your bathroom, go find your own bathroom." Wanda and I retreat back to the hall, run to our lockers as the mod tone sounds and just make it to class.

§   §   §

When Josh was five, his older sister pulled him in a wagon up and down their street. "Close your eyes," said his sister, as she walked with the wagon behind her. "We are now entering Atlantis."

Josh asked what Atlantis is like, and she told him. Then they left Atlantis and traveled to a place in France, where ("Don't look," she warned) the naked ladies dance and then to Mars where the ladies (according to the sister) smoke cigars.

In both of these faraway lands, Josh was titillated to hear, the men wear bikinis and the children drink martinis. Imagine that! Josh did. He wanted to go to these places one day and open his eyes.

§   §   §

"Did someone write #23 as a joke?"

"What do you mean, a joke? I think it's a very good poem."

"You can't put McDonald's in a poem."

"Why not? Maybe there's something inspiring about McDonald's to this person. Don't be a poetry snob."

"I'm not saying McDonald's is bad! I love

McDonald's! It just sounds like a commercial to talk about McDonald's in a poem."

"Maybe commercials are all little poems."

"I think not."

§   §   §

"I heard from Talya that Archimage has Chinese flats in maroon velvet."

"Well then let's get right over there before every female in Galaxy descends upon Monroe Avenue and they run out of our size!"

Between the two of us, Wanda and I have seven pairs of these thin cloth Alice-In-Wonderland shoes: black, black velvet, green, green velvet, white, pink, and blue. They are the cheapest shoes in the world – eight dollars a pair at Archimage – but you have to know your size in Chinese. Wanda and I wear a thirty-eight.

§   §   §

Here is how Ernie and I met: he sat next to me in tenth grade chemistry. (Not on purpose – we had assigned seats.) Another girl, April, liked Ernie and wanted to go out with him, so she asked me to ask Ernie if he liked her. Ernie was wearing the ugliest shirt I had ever seen. It was deliberately ugly, like it was his private joke on the world that he would make everyone look at this shirt, which was terry cloth with pink and yellow paramecium shapes on a pale green background. (He still wears it on special occasions.)

During class, Ernie hummed "Life in the Fast Lane" and never looked to the right or left. At first I wasn't sure who was humming. I meant to ask him if he liked April, really, I did, but I was too intimidated by that shirt.

By eleventh grade, April had forgotten that Ernie ever existed, and I had developed a ridiculous crush on him in a sudden lump of emotion that rose in me when I saw him one day riding his bicycle: his red hair, his soccer sneakers, his freckly neck.

I walked with him in the hall, pretending I had to go his direction. I mentioned, casually, that I didn't have a date for Homecoming. I said I liked his jacket; I started going to his soccer games after school and just standing there for a while, the only spectator sometimes, just for five minutes or so, maybe waving at him as I left. He got the hint and asked me to the dance, and I smiled and said yes in a surprised way as though he had thought of falling in love with me all on his own.

I have no explanation for this. I was insane. He was the cutest funniest best boy in the school and when we danced in the gym it was better than *Pretty in Pink*, it was better than *Sixteen Candles*, it was like writing the best poem of my entire life.

§   §   §

Hey guys! How bout if we sell t-shirtss for teh fund raeser!!

-Ernie

No

No

No Way

Ernie you're an idiot

This is the real Ernie and I want you to knwo I ded not type the above.

--The Real Ernie

Ernie you are a beg liar I can recogneze your destinctive typing errors anywhere you always type e's for e's I mean e's for i's oops et looks leke E do that too sometemes

-- Anonyjmous

Why no t-shirts? I like the idea\

No!

This is the Wandora Unit typing. We say that Galaxy should not sell t-shirst and the reason we think that is that every body else sells t-shirts . In Even Cowgirls Get the Blues by Tom Robbins this guru kind of guy teaches his disciples great widsom and they get all excited and ask him to be the president of their club and he says 'Does your club have a name?' yes of course 'Does your club have banners?' yes 'And bumper stickers?' yes and 'And slogans?' yes yes 'Then I have taught younothing' says

the guru and that 's how the Wandora Unit
feels about t-shirts.
The Wandora Unit is just upset because no
t-shirt would fit its double tosro four arms!
The Wandora Unet might look cute in half a
t-shert
The Wandora Unit might pop you one Ernie

§   §   §

Chapter XXVII: In Which Wanda and I, On Our Way To
School at 6:57 in the Morning, Discuss School Cliques:

"You know, I've never wanted to be a cheerleader
or a slabby or a happy buncher, but sometimes, just once
in a while, I do wish I had, like, bright purple hair," I say
to Wanda.

"Ugh, you can *not* think that – those bohemian types
are the worst! It's like in that poem: 'all the nonconformists
are doing it.' They have that neon hair to cover up their
empty heads!"

"I know, I know, but still, it does take a certain kind
of bravery, even if it is stupid, to dress that way. I'm not
saying I'd *do* it, just that I admire it. I'd rather be in the
bohemian crowd than hang out smoking cigarettes at the
slab or have all that happy-bunch school spirit."

"Okay, well, if we're confessing, I sometimes want
Benetton sweaters. But that doesn't mean it's right."

"Hey, did I tell you what Lana said?"

"What?"

"I asked her why the cheerleaders only cheer for boys' teams and never for girls' teams and Lana says, get this, she says, 'What, do you think we're lesbians or something?'"

Wanda stops walking, sighs, shakes her head, plunges an imaginary sword into her gut.

§   §   §

The goal in the U.S right now, it seems to me, is to train intelligent, well-educated people to speak stupidly so they can be more popular.

– Kurt Vonnegut

§   §   §

Earlier today, Wanda and I used my house key to carve into a picnic table at Cobb's Hill: "Wanda and Dora were here, Josh and Simon weren't." Wanda and I wanted to walk to Cobb's Hill; Josh and Simon wanted to ride bikes; Josh and Simon said we were dumb. So Wanda and I started walking and Josh and Simon followed on their bikes just behind us at about three miles per hour, but once they got to the reservoir they wouldn't talk to us and they kept not talking until hours later they followed us home and now we are in my kitchen and they are drinking all the grape juice. And they want to play Atari even though we are supposed to be too mature for that.

§   §   §

Life sucks, and then you die

– Tom's band

Life is like a grapefruit:
It's round, yellow, and it has seeds

– Ray

§   §   §

I frequently find myself using the *never* construction in conversations with Wanda. "I will never dye my hair" "I could never cheat on a boyfriend – I would just break up with the guy if I wanted to be with somebody else." "I don't think it's possible to love two people at one time...at least I never could."

Perhaps I am demanding to be heard, because Wanda is so sure of her own future ("My wedding will be in yellow and gray," or "I plan to be a professor and spend my vacations on a horse farm in Vermont") that I want to convince the both of us that my future is also, in some way, set.

Yet the proclamations insistently came out in the negative: "I will never eat sushi" "I will never wear a bikini, even if I'm skinny enough, which I will never be."

The promises we make together include "We will always be friends," "We will never stop talking to each other this way," and "We will always know what is going on in each other's lives better than anyone else, even if we get married we will understand each other better than our husbands understand us."

§   §   §

The hours that Wanda and I have spent together can be distilled – amateurishly, like the moonshine in *The Dukes of Hazzard* – into this or that discreet moment during which the two of us are truly of one mind. We both feel an ache, recognizing the beauty of dusk in my kitchen window. We drink ice water from clear blue cut glass goblets. And there is the pleasure of reading books on Wanda's couch until we both fall asleep.

I have started writing a story to remind myself that there is such a thing as truth. I can't tell what the truth is, but if I put enough words down it will be in there. What is happening to our friendship? Why don't we want to be friends, the way we used to be, now that we are leaving high school? What happened? Did something happen? Or is this just what it means to be grown up, to be satisfied with different kinds of friendships, not to want a best friend, a confidante for everything?

§   §   §

Josh speaks:

It's because of me that they had their big argument,

and I'm really sorry about it. Dora and I used to call each other every day after *Thundercats*, plus all that driving around together we used to do after play rehearsals – when I think about it, it was pretty romantic. I mean, I know she was going out with Ernie and everything, but still.

I'm not saying I knew she liked me, I mean *like* liked me, I just realize now that I was callous. She hated having secrets kept from her, and I knew that, but I thought at the time it was better not to tell her, that I could protect her. About both the physics thing and my, you know, crush.

The thing about both of them is, they let their imaginations run wild. They can't accept things as they are – they always want things to be *more*. Like, they always remember their dreams in vivid detail, and they tell each other all about them. I wanted to be part of that, but I never remember my dreams, or if I do it's a dream that I forgot my locker combination or something totally mundane like that.

§   §   §

"#29 is, like, totally sexual. Just listen to it – 'He asked me if, as he was my friend, he could eat my blueberries...'"

"You're reading it sexually on purpose!"

"I can't help it! It just comes out that way!"

"Well now, Galaxians," interrupts Norris in his imperious voice, "Please remember that the tone of voice heard in that rendition is probably not the intended tone of the poet."

Everyone at the meeting snickers. Yvonne Pie asks if the writer is male or female. I ask why that would matter.

"Well, blueberries seem like a feminine symbol."

"And she's talking to a male so that makes sense."

"No, that doesn't prove anything –"

"I think it's about friendship, not sex. Not even love!"

"Boring."

"I think the blueberries stand for the writer's innermost self."

"That makes sense too."

"Or they could just be actual blueberries."

"Freud would say..."

"Whether it's a love poem or a friendship poem, it's still about asking and giving, though, right?" I say. (I am trying to support Wanda, who in fact wrote the poem, and is too mortified by all this sexual innuendo to speak for herself) "I mean the blueberries are a gift that must be requested, and so the request becomes another gift."

"Hey, deep."

"Anybody want my blueberries? They're juicy and ripe!"

"Oh, shut up."

"It does rhyme in one place though."

"That doesn't necessarily make it a bad poem."

"Yes it does. Rhyming is for sissies."

"I think that's an accidental rhyme anyway."

"So what is it about?"

"The blueberries could stand for death..."

§   §   §

Ernie finds things. Money, usually, dimes, quarters; he once found a twenty dollar bill floating in the ocean. He also finds other people's contact lenses (they stand completely still, whining about how much it will cost to buy a replacement for the tiny clear plastic mangled thing that turns out to be caught in their sleeve or their hair). Keys, mittens, maps, notebooks – anything lost, Ernie will pick it up by chance.

Ernie has Spanish mods 14 - 16 in room 306, in the same room where I have math earlier in the day. He habitually checks around my desk for any remains of me. (He knows where I sit because he has mods 7 - 9 free and he sometimes waits for me in the hall outside the classroom so we can go to lunch together.)

Usually there is nothing, but occasionally he finds a pen, white with a blue cap, lying in the wooden trough of the desk. Ernie takes these pens and keeps them for himself. I start out each month with six or eight, and by the end, he has stolen half of them.

One day, mooching around my desk hoping for a pen since he once again forgot his, Ernie finds a gold hoop earring lying on the floor next to the front chair leg. He twirled it on his fingers. It is so familiar to him – I wear these earrings every day – they are my favorite earrings, practically the only ones I ever wear.

After school in the Galaxy room, Ernie holds the earring out to me, not saying a word.

I instinctively grab at my earlobes, find nothing

hanging from the left one. "Hey, where did you get that? My earring! I would die without that earring!" My voice, as it always does when I am excited, becomes progressively louder and higher. "I didn't even know it was missing! How did you find it? Where was it?"

The earring is a little halo in his hand. I reach for it, and Ernie shrugs. He's happy to supply me with the things I don't know I need.

§   §   §

"Today let's walk up Monroe and go shopping in the city at Archimage, After Eden, the music store, and the Brown Bag Bookshop, and then let's go to the food co-op and buy some strange kind of organic bread and eat it at Cobb's Hill," I say to Wanda. "How does that sound?"

"Wonderful," answers Wanda. "Just give me five minutes."

The bread we buy is called "Molasses Wheat" and it's delicious under a tree by the reservoir.

§   §   §

Chapter XXVIII: In Which Wanda and I, In the Galaxy Room By Ourselves Mods 17-19, Discuss Our Arms Hurting:

"You know, I can't understand it, but I have this weird pain in my upper arms, and it hurts to raise them over my head."

"That is very weird. I have the same thing! Are we

doing something in gym class that would cause this?"

"I don't think so. What are we doing, anyway, volleyball, right?"

"Yes, co-ed."

"I get the shivers when that cardboard wall between our side of the gym and the boys' side starts bending back."

"I like having co-ed gym, but not for things I can't play like volleyball."

"Anyhow it can't be from volleyball. It's something else."

"Well what have we both been doing lately?"

"Let's see. It can't be from typing on the scroll because we don't do that enough. Could it be from chicken fights?"

"I don't think so."

"Well I give up."

"We can't give up! Let's ask everyone we know until we figure it out."

§ § §

The thing with Ernie is, we do not really have much in common. You'd think I would go out with someone who likes to write poems, or at least read them. All Ernie ever says about my poems is "They're very well written."

He doesn't want to talk about books with me, or do intellectual things. He just likes me and wants to be with me. As far as I can tell, he doesn't know why, and he doesn't care. He takes me for granted in the nicest possible way.

Maybe that is why, when I break up with him, something in both of us gets ruined forever. Something maybe we didn't even know was ruinable.

In most novels, the meaning of the love relationship is obvious. Like, if the girlfriend wears "a proper dress that falls exactly one inch below her knees," you know she's no good. Two chapters later the main character is going to dump her. But in my actual life I don't know the meaning of the love relationship. Most of the time I totally love Ernie. Other times I think I should hit myself on the head with a frying pan for even considering that lunk. Shouldn't it be obvious, whether or not we belong together? Like in the Rickie Lee Jones song? Except even in that song she's trying to convince him: "Don't you know that we belong together, we belong together, we belong together." Maybe when I'm older this will all become clear. But what if it doesn't, ever? What if you never know if you are doing the right thing, or if you did the right thing, or if you are about to make a huge mistake?

§   §   §

"Why are we friends?" I ask Wanda, knowing she will have an answer.

"Because we bring out the best selves of each other. Because we *are* the best selves of each other. Also we live on the same street and we have Simon and Josh and Ray."

"But even without them, we would still be best friends."

"Also, it's very lucky that we both have boyfriends at the same time. Isn't it great, finally having a boyfriend?"

"Yeah, I love it. I love that we're having these experiences together, even if we're not actually in the same room at the time, you know? But are Ernie and Norris really helping our friendship?"

"No, Ernie and Norris are hurting. But a lack of Ernie and Norris would hurt our friendship even more."

"Because we would fall into the trap of if-I-had-a-boyfriend-my-life-would-be-perfect," I say, because Wanda and I have both fallen into this trap before.

"I wish we could put Ernie and Norris in a back room, and just take them out when we wanted them – moonlit nights or whatever."

"I don't think they would like that very much, though."

"Well, exactly, that's why we can't. Too bad though. It would be so much more convenient."

"Hey, let's make a pact."

"What kind of pact?" asks Wanda, already warming to the idea.

"I don't know, something with…underwear!"

We make a pact to get rid of all our old, ratty pairs. We decide it will improve our poetry. "We have to start from the bottom up," I say, giggling.

We throw all of our ripped, stained, holey pairs of underwear away – twenty pairs of teenage female underwear go into the garbage on our street that afternoon.

§　§　§

"Well, #33 is obviously about love."

"But some kind of abnormal love."

"Abnormal how?"

"Well it's all *sticky*! That's not normal. I mean, 'silken strangleholds'?"

"But that is how love is."

"Maybe for you."

"Have you ever been in love?"

"Now, now, let's not get personal. Back to the poem please. What do you think it means that they are 'against the future'?"

"I thought that meant just, you know, standing there looking at the future, not knowing what it will be."

"I think it's a nuclear war."

"A nuclear war? Where in the world did you get that?"

"Well, look at that last line. The sky is on fire!"

"He's not...oh, the *sky*. I thought you said *this guy*."

"Maybe he is on fire."

"That would make the poem more interesting."

"I think it's interesting enough. I think they're against the future because they know the future will destroy their love, nuclear war or not."

"That's corny."

"Just because something is corny doesn't mean it isn't true."

"What about the title?"

"Hey, that goes together! Loom, like a weaving loom, and also like the future looms before them!"

"Here we have an example of good ambiguity."

"I think it's ambiguous ambiguity."

"I really like this poem."

"We're not allowed to say if we like it or not."

"I feel ambiguous about it."

"Ambivalent. You feel ambivalent."

"How can you be sure? Maybe I feel ambiguous. Maybe I feel ambiguous about everything. Or maybe not."

§   §   §

Chapter XCVI: In Which Wanda and I Figure Out Why Our Arms Hurt:

"Dora, I think I figured it out."

"What?"

"Why our arms hurt."

"Well, why?"

"They always hurt on Sundays and Mondays especially, right?"

"Yeah, so, don't keep me in suspense, what is it?"

"I think it's from, uh, kissing."

"What do you mean, kissing? Why would that make our arms...oh! You think – from making out? From having our arms up and around..."

We each raise our arms around phantom shoulders, tilt our heads back.

"Yep, that's it all right. That makes my arms hurt even more. You solved it. How did you realize?"

"Well, last night I was complaining about it to my mother, and..."

"Your mother said 'Well, dear, have you been making out a lot lately?'"

"Yeah, exactly. No, *duh*, it's just that I showed her the position they hurt the worst in, and she said maybe I'd been doing too much waltzing, that could do it, and there it was."

"Waltzing, huh."

"That's a nice term for it, isn't it? Maybe from now on we should say 'I really like waltzing' or 'would you care to waltz, my love?'"

"And then they can say 'I'm sorry, my sweet, but all this waltzing is giving me a hard-on and soon I shall suffer from blue balls.'"

"Hey, that's good, waltzing, balls."

"Well, as you may have heard, I'd like to be a writer someday."

§ § §

"Boy, do I not get #37."

"You mean 'To Jar'? Me neither."

"It makes me think of that assignment in third grade, when you stick a caterpillar in a jar and wait for it to build a cocoon and everything."

"Mine died."

"I don't think it has anything to do with caterpillars, I think it's about suicide."

"Every poem in here is about suicide."

"Well, whose fault is that? I mean we get to say what

the poem means, and we always think it's suicide. It seems to me that we're forcing our will upon the poem."

"But it is a fact that aspiring poets often want to kill themselves."

"But aspiring suicides are seldom poets."

"Don't be gruesome – let's read it again!"

§   §   §

I usually call Josh up after school at 4:00 in the afternoon directly after *Thundercats* on cable TV. When he answers the phone – generally munching on something, raw spaghetti, Doritos, pretzels, crunchy peanut butter in a spoon – I recite for him the moral I perceive as emerging from the episode we have just watched in our separate living rooms.

"Lying is bad." "Cheating is bad." "Mutants are stupid, and that is why they are evil." "Evil never triumphs."

Josh responds variously. He seldom disagrees with my interpretation, but often requires a more delicate reading of the text: "But when Lion-O left the Thunderkittens alone to take care of themselves, wasn't he sending a mixed message? The balance of nurturing and abandonment here is problematic. Couldn't Panthro or Cheetara have looked after the kittens for an hour?"

"The moral is that the kittens should be independent, but not too independent. Lion-O was acting as a responsible father-figure – he was encouraging the twins' independence, but he overestimated their development, to almost dire consequences."

"So when are you coming over?"

"Now."

I get on my bike and ride the two miles to Josh's house. I do not use the kickstand upon arrival, just dump the bike on its side in his front yard. All we ever do at his house is sit around in the TV room, but it's just the two of us, which doesn't happen often.

§   §   §

given: We are the smartest, the srmartest in the entire school
PROVE: we can do whatever we want

eeewwww math
Who says we'Re the smartest in the school?
that's the GIVEN
oh, fine, it's the given. Okay we are the smartst. Even if we kint speel

one time I was caught during closed mods in the hall by the vice principal and i didnt' get in trouble at all I told him I had nowhere to go because I didn't want to go the cafeteria and thenn he just let me go and I did not get detention. Yeah!

All I know is theres this big huge cheating ring going on in AP Physics and no one seems to care not even the teacher.

Thes is a nerd topic for nerds everyone knows
who runs the school and et esn't us so we
should no t delude ourselves.
I walked out of the cafeteria with a can of
hi-C and Mrs. Philbin saw me and told me I had
detention for a week so I guess thatDISPROVES
the entire theory
or maybe you just aren't the msartest in the
school

§   §   §

In our one mod for lunch (mod 10) Josh, Ernie, and
I take exactly eighteen minutes to walk to Murray's for
pizza bagels, scarf them down, and hurry back to school.
(Wanda has lunch mod 13, so she eats with Ray and
Simon.) Ernie eats really fast so he has time to play Time
Pilot, which Josh and I agree is one of the dumbest video
games we've ever seen, but Ernie loves it. He is probably
the only person to play it, so he usually gets the high score.
Today he gets four high scores in a row and types for the
initials

843, 670	EBS
832, 520	ADD
811, 980	DGN
807, 240	4VR

to leave proof of his love for me. Ernest Brett Goldstein Plus Dora Gail Nussbaum Forever. Isn't that the most romantic thing you've ever heard?

Ernie's soccer number is thirty-two, and that has become my favorite number. I do my sit ups and push ups and leg lifts in multiples of thirty-two, and the thirty-two in my locker combination is clearly a sign that Ernie and I belong together.

§ § §

"Why are we wearing bras on our heads?"

"Ceremonial purposes."

After seeing *Weird Science,* Wanda and I are now in love with Anthony Michael Hall because he is so geeky and lovable. It makes us proud that we have a crush on a geek – other girls like the usual action heroes, Tom Cruise and such. Wanda and I refuse to like anyone typical and forge a geeky unrequited love of our own.

There is this girl named Karen Sung in my math class. She is a closet poet; she doesn't show anyone her stuff or go to Galaxy meetings. I found out she writes, though, because her boyfriend, Mike Nunzio, is in my homeroom (Nussbaum and Nunzio – homerooms are alphabetical) and when I was hanging posters asking for submissions to Galaxy, Mike sidled up to me and whispered that I should ask his girlfriend. He said Karen won't even show anything to him, but he suspects she is good.

So, I asked her. She gave me only one poem. It is well-nigh incomprehensible, and reading it makes me wonder if Karen is brilliant or just needs therapy. We'll see what kind of reception it gets at the meeting.

§   §   §

"Any feelings on #40? The poem entitled 'Romance Novels'?"

"Strange."

"Elusive."

"You love the word elusive."

"But in this case it really is."

"What does that mean, the carved out hole?"

"Well, if the monsters are romance novels, maybe it's like those trashy novels with the hole in the front cover illustration?"

"Yeah, and the page edges dyed different colors, like it says."

Nobody at the meeting really gets it, and the Galaxy members suspect the author doesn't even know what it's about.

§   §   §

"If I can jump this puddle, she likes me." Josh is on his way home from school. It has been raining all week, and he feels like he can't remember what the weather is like when it's not raining. There are puddles all over the sidewalk. No one is looking, but Josh is talking to himself and leaping over them, taking a few running steps beforehand. "If I can jump this one, she definitely likes me. Well, best two out of three."

When he gets home he will do his math homework and at the same time watch *Thundercats* and eat a bowl of Cap'n Crunch (with Crunchberries). Then, while he writes up his physics lab report, he will talk to me on the phone, as if we don't see enough of each other all day in the Galaxy room.

§   §   §

RUMORS

```
Norres got a B in one class.
THat is a blatnant lie!!!   --Norris
Glaxy  is  going  to  cost  $5.00  an  issue
thisyear.
Yvonnte tqakes LSXD I mean LSD
```

THe Wandora Unet are lesbean lovers

Josh likes Air SUpply

Don't make me laugh! -Josh

Ernie wishes Dora andWanda were lesbien lovers

How can a unit be loverrs -wouldnt' that be like massturbation?

Ms. Green's cat is pregnatn by the principal's cat

TOms' band mihgt ghet a recordign contract.

Norrris has a large ego

that's not a rumor that's a FACT

Ray eats lunch with his grandmsother every Teusday

That's an exciting rumour

Moni ca has a tattoo on her butt of Baby Huey

who is baby Huey?

a big bird in a diaper (I looked at Monica'sbutt)

anorexia runs rampant throught the Girsls Track Team and soemething should be done about it this is serious

Heather SMith is a virgin

a sophomoer got beat up in the cafeteria bec use he took someone's frienchfires I mean french fries not fires

there's a fire in the cafateria it startted in the french fries

BIll Brunhueber sometimes talks

Ms. Green is writeing a book about us

```
Ms. Green is enganged to be married
Ms green is about to lose her job becaues of
how loud we are
Linda Schuman had a nose job   everybody know
s that
```

§   §   §

Chapter XXVII: In Which Wanda and I, On Our Way to School at 7:02 in the Morning, Discuss the Nature of Love:

It is December in Rochester; the Wandora Unit dresses in many layers for our walk to school. We are each wearing two pairs of socks, knee high boots, long underwear under our skirts, a tank top, a turtleneck, a wool sweater, a long coat, scarf, hat, thin gloves, and thick mittens. Our talk is punctuated with "Brrrr" sounds.

"I mean obviously I love Norris, but I think I would have to love him differently if I didn't have you. I mean Norris doesn't want to *talk* about things."

"Well what does he want to do?"

"Well," Wanda says looking sheepish, "Honestly, we spend a lot of time just looking in each other's eyes."

"That's romantic."

"Yeah, I guess."

"If I look in Ernie's eyes for very long I want to kiss him, or else I want to kill him."

"I never want to kill Norris."

"I know."

Upon arriving at school we stride down the long hall and then split up at the stairs to go to our separate lockers. There we perform an accidentally synchronized dance: we each open the locker, remove our shoes from our backpacks and place them together on the floor, stuff the backpack in the locker and, hanging on to the locker door, balance on our left feet to yank off our right boots, the doubly-socked feet gracefully emerging like clean little babies. We each slip our right feet into our right shoes and remove the left boots the same way. The boots, wet with melting snow, go on the bottom of the lockers with a clang.

§ § §

Such pimples! Such hardons!
Such moody loves!
And thus they grew like giggling fir trees.

— **Frank O'Hara, "Blocks"**

§ § §

Chapter XI: In Which Ms. Green Defines the Purpose of Poetry:

"If you don't like these poems, write some of your own," says Ms. Green in AP English. Besides the required poems in the textbook (Shakespeare, Emily Dickinson, William Carlos Williams), she makes us read Frank O'Hara, Nikki Giovanni, Audre Lorde, Tu Fu, Rilke, Lorca, Rimbaud, Anne Sexton, Wallace Stevens, Mayakovsky.

She has no patience with laziness. "You are all a bunch of sloths! You don't like reading Dante because it is too hard? Imagine *writing* those books – now *that* is hard. Turn in your papers on Monday, and no spiral notebook squigglies! Anyone handing in a paper with spiral squigglies will lose half a grade. I mean it."

§   §   §

When I was nine, I walked through doorways hoping to emerge from this room or that room into an imaginary land. I thought I was like Dorothy, Alice, Lucy and the wardrobe. There was a place near the library where two trees had grown together to make an arch, and this was my most hopeful spot – I closed my eyes as I walked through, or rode through on my bike no-handed to try to make the magic work. I even occasionally held still in the space between the trees, giving the other dimension a chance to let me in.

At the same time, miles and miles away, Wanda waited in the middle of a New Hampshire meadow for alien ships to come down and get her and take her away to distant planets. Our secret dreams at age nine were somewhat different, but basically the same: we wanted to go somewhere else.

By the time we moved to Brighton, both of us had stopped doing anything about leaving this world. But we hadn't stopped thinking about it. Closets beckoned; empty fields glowed.

§ § §

RING

"Hello."

"You should always be yourself, Josh."

"Geez, the credits are still on. Can't you wait?"

"I can reach the phone from the couch."

"You know, I think I've seen this episode four times."

"No, it's just that Be Yourself is always the moral."

"Sometimes it's Trust Your Parents."

"True, true."

"How's Eeeeeernie?"

"You don't have to say it like that. What are you eating?"

"Doritos."

"Ernie is fine. How's your girlfriend?"

"Very funny."

"Well, who knows, you could have met someone on the way home from school."

"Yeah, just because you think you have the romance of the century doesn't mean the rest of us can be so lucky."

"I don't think I have the romance of the century."

"What's wrong with Ernie?"

"Nothing. He – nothing."

"Come on, what?"

"Nothing."

"You know you're going to tell me."

"I don't know any such thing. Everything's fine, it's just – does your mother buy your clothes?"

"Ernie's mother still buys his clothes?"

"Yeah. I don't mean just underwear and socks either – she buys it *all*. Ernie has never bought himself a pair of pants or a shirt or *anything*."

"No wonder he dresses like a putz."

"He doesn't dress like a putz."

"Have it your way."

"Listen, Wanda's here, we're going to Monroe Avenue."

"Buy me something nice for Hanukkah."

"Okay, bye."

"Bye."

PART II

At the Galaxy Christmas/Hanukkah/Solstice party at Simon's house, six people are standing in doorways. Monica Braverman is showing everyone the magic arm trick: you stand in a doorway and press your arms against the walls, as if your arms are wings and you are trying to raise them, and count to twenty, and then take a step forward out of the doorway and your arms miraculously rise up on either side of you. Wanda and I try it, and it works! But you have to press really hard, as hard as you possibly can.

Simon is breakdancing on the living room floor, or pretending to anyway. He can sort of do the moonwalk. He and Josh throw "energy" back and forth, robotically undulating their bodies, but when Simon throws the energy to Melissa Klein, she carefully places it under one of the couch cushions and the breakdancing ends.

Josh does the mambo by himself. He is not half bad. He has lent me his wristwatch again until further notice. Wanda and I are just wandering around this party, not settling anywhere.

Carl Jacobs sits by himself in a chair on the cold side porch. He is depressed. Carl Jacobs often becomes depressed at parties, especially if there are girls around. He sighs, looks sad, tells stories about his horrible parents and how awful everything is in his family.

The girl he draws into his patheticness at this

party, Judy Gage, has a much worse family than Carl, but she comes onto the porch, asks what's wrong, nods sympathetically, holds Carl's hand and tells him she'll always be his friend. But no one can listen to these stories for long! Especially since he makes most of them up.

In the kitchen, while the radio plays 10,000 Maniacs, Yvonne Pie teaches Gina Marcone how to hyperventilate. "No, really, it's fun! You can get high from this!"

Wanda and I get involved in the chicken fights in the back yard. The snow is three feet deep. We climb on top of the shoulders of Ernie and Norris and then fall almost simultaneously, lie tangled in our own bodies, laughing. The ski tags hanging from the zipper of Norris's jacket glint in the moonlight. To get up out of the snow Wanda and I sit back to back, link elbows, push against each other to stand. We unlink, separate, walk in opposite directions. Climb back onto the boys to do more battle. It is hard to say: are we fighting? Or are we embracing? Chicken fights are ambiguous, like good poetry. Exhausting, and symbolic.

§   §   §

At Galaxy meeting at Wanda's house, Wanda and I ask Simon "May we take your coat?" and then we take it and hide it in the basement and when he wants it back at the end of the meeting, we exclaim "Well you *said* we could take it!"

We are HILARIOUS.

Stream-of-Consciousness Assignment

water cold on my skin the sun huge taking up the whole sky eaten by the water gray stones sharp on our bare feet my friends spread out yelling falling in the cold cold water at one place in the creek a short waterfall we can stand inside it water filling us up my bathing suit black three years old going ratty shoulder straps about to snap the waterfall almost takes my suit off I hold on grabbing myself did anyone see? we know each other well enough but not too well I never kissed any of them except once playing stupid spin the bottle at a stupid party kissed Josh after knowing him for years it was a sweet kiss very short we were sitting on the floor the rug felt scratchy and the house was warm outside it was snowing we skidded on the way over on purpose in one of those circular driveways did I like it? It scared me also was exhilarating I was in the backseat surrounded by love I could feel with my hands in the dark our faces now in the bright hot sun water dripping off us playing in the water like seals at the north pole on TV what a perfect day except for when I sprained my finger and also they were mad at me because I brought Ernie I could tell they wished he wasn't there I agreed with them actually except for the part at the top of the hike with the big flat stones and no one else around

"Where's Dora?"

"In the bathroom, nosy."

"What's she doing in there? When will she be back?"

"Geez, Ernie, probably she's peeing."

§ § §

Hello my name is Tom and I am a drummer in a band. I heard that poeple in this roomare CREATIVE and my band needs a name. Please help us and think of a name for the band.

how about The Issues?

How about The Tissues?

What kind of music is it? If it's heavy metal, you should be called Emasculator.

The Flannery O'Connors

The Frank O'Haras

Sometimes Y

The Poems

The Poetries

The Poa Trees

White Sloth

The Clyde Peelings

    (aFter Clyde Peeling's Rpseptile Land on Rouute 15)

The Route 15's

The Typewriters
Wizard
The Brunheubers
The Cliches
Mud
Unicorn
Vomit
The Rays
Ray can't you th ink of anything besides
yourself?
The Wandas
Oh Great Ray that makes up for it thanks
The Egos
The Ids
TheCommunists
Industrial Revolution
The Ms's   that's too hard to pronounce
how about The Mizzes
The Velmas
Fluffy Surprise
The Oafs
Tom's Band
The Yeast Infections
The Yogurts

§   §   §

I say, "Let's go ice skating at Manhattan Square
Park and then come back to my house and play the piano
and drink hot chocolate."

"You always have such good ideas of what to do," says Wanda.

§   §   §

Simon speaks:

I think it started happening long before senior year, actually. Ray and I used to talk about this a lot. We all used to hang out in a group – Ray, me, Josh, Dora and Wanda – and we were all just buddies, you know? We used to ride our bikes and rent movies and stuff. I mean sure, once in a while we got the hots for each other, but we never did anything about it. Except Josh of course. But anyway, some time during junior year there was this change. Josh and I stopped hanging out together so much, because Ray and I were doing track after school. And around the same time, Dora and Wanda starting acting strange. If you ask me, they went a little crazy. It was like they *had* to be the same. See, I think they never really were. Wanda was always, like, more refined – Dora was kind of tough, or at least she wanted to be tough. And Wanda had more, you know, traditional views of sex, marriage, all that crap. Dora was always more likely to just run off with some guy. But the *point* I'm trying to make here is, they *weren't* the same, they just *pretended* to be, as if that would make them better friends.

It was like they had some kind of competition going with the whole world, that no one could be as close friends as they were. Of course it wore off after a while, but to my mind, the trouble began when they started that Wandora Unit bullshit, which was bullshit, because they were never one unit at all.

§ § §

Poetry is life distilled.

– Gwendolyn Brooks

The poet's pleasure in finding ingenious ways to enclose her secrets should be matched by the reader's pleasure in unlocking and revealing these secrets.

– Diane Wakoski

§ § §

"#60, 'Hungary Like the Wolf,' if I am not mistaken, is not a poem by someone in Brighton High School, but rather the lyrics to a song by Duran Duran."

"Except someone does not know how to spell the word *hungry*."

"You mean that's not how you spell it?" Ray, the typist, has given himself away.

"Do you guys seriously expect us to discuss this?"

"Why not? It's a poem, isn't it?"

"And you want to know the deep meaning of it, right? Well I'll tell you the deep meaning..."

"Simon, we know you do not like Duran Duran."

"The deep meaning of this poem is that the speaker feels so much desire that he or she actually feels him - or her - self to be a foreign country, i.e., Hungary."

 "Typos can be poetry!"

§   §   §

In homeroom I look out the window, watching the buses leave until my husband arrives.

Matthew Nussbaum is not, of course, my real husband. He is the captain of the football team (wowee) but on occasion he deigns to comply with my little joke – our homeroom teacher, noticing we had the same last name, once asked whether we were brother and sister. I replied, "No, he's my husband," forgetting that at 7:15 in the morning most people have not yet roused a sense of humor.

Matt is dumb but not as dumb as he might be, and I have a feeling he might be writing poems, stashing them in his football helmet or in his cleats...or in his jock!

Every morning we banter like talk show hosts. This morning Matt asks me "Did you get in a fight with a lawnmower, huh, huh?" a deserved comment on my new haircut, which makes me look like a punk squirrel.

I have no clever comeback. I know my haircut is terrible, but since I will never be beautiful, what's the point of bothering? The best I can hope for is interesting-looking.

I ask if Brighton won the last football game, not

because I care but because I am trying to point out to Matt that I don't know the answer, that not everyone pays close attention to school sports. I doubt he gets the message, since he gives me a detailed description of the near-triumph of his team.

§   §   §

"I love #65!"

"Yvonne, please."

"Why can't I say if I love it?"

"What do you think it means?"

"I have no idea! But it sounds great. Out onto the morning damp green bare feet found dew..."

"Yes, we've all read it."

"What's an odyssey?"

"A long journey."

"Like...life!"

"Like, her day at school."

"If she had put on a different shirt that morning, would she have had a different day?"

"We've already had this whole discussion on the scroll."

§   §   §

"Where's Wanda?" asks Josh.

"She's in the cafeteria bringing me some french fries."

"Why isn't she bringing me anything?"

"Maybe because you never have any money, and besides which, you just had lunch! Why are you still hungry?"

"I'm not, really, I just wanted Wanda to bring me something to show how much she worships me."

"I'll tell you what, dumb head, as a symbol of how much Wanda and I adore you, I'll give you half a fry."

"That's cool."

§   §   §

At Galaxy meeting at Yvonne Pie's house all the poems are on old-fashioned computer paper with holes in a perforated stripe down each side. Ray rips the holes off all the pages and makes himself a headdress out of the strings of paper.

§   §   §

RING
"Hello."
"Hey, where's my call for the day?"
"Oh, uh, it's just that – Ernie's here."
"See ya."
"No, Josh, I mean – what was the moral?"
"I thought old Ernie had soccer practice."
"Canceled. Too much snow."
"Mmm."
"So what was the moral?"
"Be yourself, like always. And if other people don't

like the real you, you don't want to be friends with them anyway."

"Interesting twist. Listen –"

"Yeah, so I'll see you around Dora, have a good time with Ernie."

"Yeah, okay, see you tomorrow."

§   §   §

"What do you really think of me – I mean *really*."

"You *are* me."

It is like Wanda and I are always listening to the same music, our earphones plugged in to the same jack. (I tried this with Ernie once, on his bus: we argued about what station to listen to and I ended up just looking out the window.)

§   §   §

Galaxy is attending the Empire State School Publications Association banquet at Syracuse University. All the editors will sleep on the couches of nice people's houses. The bus ride lasts two hours and Ernie is not there, Norris is not there, and Ray has the flu.

On the way to the ESSPA event, Simon, Josh, Wanda and I get rowdy in the back, singing "9,999 Bottles of Beer On the Wall" and generally making pains of ourselves. The kids from the newspaper ignore us and continue interviewing each other. The yearbook gang roll their eyes and take photographs of themselves. *Those Galaxy people are just too weird, and annoying besides. Why are they even attending the banquet? They aren't a real publication.*

But this is the first time in months that the Boyfriends are not present, and Wanda and I no longer even care if Galaxy wins an award. Well, only a little. We just feel happy and full of fun, and we yell poems out the window. We pick poems out of each other's hair. Poems fill the bus invisibly. For an hour and a half the poems exist only as radio waves, moving through everything in complete silence.

§   §   §

"#68 is like that other one we read, where the school ate the guy."

"I don't think school is so destructive. I think it has some good points."

"But it's more destructive than it should be. I mean half the teachers just don't care about us at all, and the ones that do, they burn out and they leave or they go crazy."

"Do you think it's really true, that school is like television?"

"I don't think it's saying school is like television. I think it's saying school turns us into televisions, that just click on and off."

"But there is hope, according to the parentheses at the end."

"Poetry will save us!"

§   §   §

"I can't *believe* we have to go to gym at 7:15."

"Even worse, play floor hockey."

"Oh no, not floor hockey! I'm *afraid* of floor hockey!"

"Well of course we're afraid of floor hockey – look at these girls – they're monsters!"

"We shouldn't have to take gym."

"Of course not, it's absurd. And floor hockey is barely a step above those awful scooters we had to ride around in middle school."

"Or crab soccer."

"Perish the thought of crab soccer from your mind."

At least we are on the same team today. We wear the blue pinneys. We get creamed by the red pinneys, who aren't averse to a little hockey stick smacking. On the other side of the folding gym wall the boys are playing basketball.

They do not have to wear pinneys because they play shirts and skins. How embarrassing for the fat boys, and the skinny boys. And the hairy boys, and the hairless. Gym is an embarrassment to almost all the boys. It would be awful to be a boy.

§　§　§

"Where's Dora?"

"She's getting more paper towels for the scroll."

§　§　§

"Wanda" and "Dora" are not easily transposed into nicknames. Perhaps that is why we do not mind the appellation "Wandora Unit" – it is the closest we can get to the inherent coolness of having a nickname.

The name vaults us to a higher plane of coolness, and we can only get there together: linguistically joined at the hip, the Wandora Unit crosses over into a kind of popularity, known-ness, in school. Ernie didn't mean to bring us closer together when he invented the term – he didn't mean to create a self-perpetuating, self-destructing monster – but that is what he did.

§   §   §

On the bus home from the ESSPA banquet in Syracuse, I sit up front with Ms. Green. Galaxy won a prize for literary content, so the mood is exuberant. We talk about form and poetry: the sestina, the rondel, the pantoum.

I yammer a mile a minute. "Why don't you teach a creative writing class? Because nobody is going to write a pantoum without being forced but it might be worth forcing someone! There should be a creative writing class at Brighton. Why isn't there one? I would take it, Wanda would take it, Josh would take it, practically everybody in Galaxy would take it, plus all the people who submit to Galaxy, this is a great idea I'm having, would you want to teach it? Of course you would. How about if I get up a petition and get everyone in Galaxy to sign it. Credit for writing poetry! Three mods in a row! It would be awesome!"

After a while, the bus driver turns around and tells me to be quiet. "Give me a break," she says, "Don't you ever shut up? I can't stand it another minute."

I am stricken, face white with embarrassment. I quickly get up and go back to my seat with Wanda. Look out the window the rest of the way home, trying not to cry. The bus driver is right. I am a pain in the ass. I *can't* ever shut up, that is the problem. I really can't. I have tried. But then when I get excited about something, or something funny happens, out comes my 800 decibel voice.

§   §   §

Sometimes I think all books should be more like that *Choose Your Own Adventure* series. If you cry all night and never recover, turn to page 106. If you embitter yourself and never trust anyone again in your entire life, turn to page 108. If Wanda understands that you just can't talk about it, turn to page 23.

I always cheated in those *Choose Your Own Adventure* books. If I decided to ride the woolly mammoth and go to page 66 but page 66 had a really short paragraph and then "the end" at the bottom, I'd tell myself that really my choice was to go back in the cave of time or whatever.

Here I am flipping around a *Choose Your Own Adventure* and it's my life and I'm acting like I can do it over until I get it right!

§ § §

When Ernie comes into the Galaxy room, I feel all the molecules of my skin, shoulders, hair, face, chest fly out to him like many tiny bees, leaving me bare to the world and happy to be bodiless, all of my self buzzing around Ernie in secret fireworks; I can hardly contain my love for him, there is no Tupperware that could hold it; I have to get up from where I am sitting and go sit somewhere closer to him, if he moves I move so I am still touching him, or at least my brain is touching him.

We can make out for hours and not think of anything but each other the whole time.

Brighton High News

WE'RE PROUD

THE PHYSICS DEPARTMENT IS PROUD TO ANNOUNCE THAT MEMBERS OF THE SENIOR AP PHYSICS CLASS ARE ACHIEVING HIGHER AVERAGES ON THE WEEKLY PRACTICE AP PHYSICS EXAMS THAN EVER BEFORE IN BRIGHTON HIGH SCHOOL. OUR CONGRATULATIONS TO THE HARD WORKING STUDENTS!

HOCKEY

THE GIRLS' FLOOR HOCKEY TEAM BEAT PITTSFORD YESTERDAY 3-2 WITH ONLY ONE MINOR INJURY TO EACH SIDE. COACH RILEY COMMENTED, "MY GIRLS SHOW EXCELLENT PROMISE. I DO BELIEVE THIS TEAM MAY BE TOUGH ENOUGH TO GO TO THE FINALS." (SEE P.4)

CHEERS TO GALAXY

BRIGHTON HIGH SCHOOL'S LITERARY MAGAZINE, GALAXY, HAS WON AN AWARD FROM THE EMPIRE STATE STUDENT PUBLICATION ASSOCIATION. "WE ARE VERY EXCITED TO SEE ALL THIS NEW TALENT," SAID ONE OF THE ESSPA JUDGES, "AND WE HOPE THE NEXT ISSUE OF GALAXY WILL BE AS IMPRESSIVE AS THIS ONE IN TERMS OF QUALITY WRITING."

GALAXY IS STILL ACCEPTING SUBMISSIONS FOR THIS YEAR'S ISSUE. PLEASE DROP OFF YOUR POETRY ON ANY SUBJECT AND IN ANY STYLE TO EDITORS WANDA LOWELL AND DORA NUSSBAUM IN THE GALAXY ROOM, LOCATED ON THE SECOND FLOOR NEXT TO THE LIBRARY.

§ § §

RING
"Hello."

"Don't try to do something dangerous on your own."

"Get help from your parents. So how was your afternoon with Ernie the studmuffin?"

"It was – it was fun."

"What did you do?"

"Oh, we – nothing much."

"Ah."

"Don't sound so knowing – it isn't often that they cancel practice."

"I know, I know."

"We had a good time."

"Good."

"…"

"…"

"What are you eating?"

"Raw spaghetti."

"Yum."

"Try it, you'd like it."

"So tell me, how'd things go with that girl from anthropology?"

"They didn't."

"Oh."

"She's sort of a dog, anyway."

"That's too bad, I really thought she liked you. Always playing with your hair."

"Well, I guess she changed her mind."

"You know, some girls have no taste."

"No kidding."

"What's that supposed to mean?"

"You know I think Ernie is a dork."

"Oh shut up Josh, you hardly know him."

"I don't have to know him. Besides, I know him well enough."

"Okay, what's wrong with him?"

"He doesn't buy his own clothes, for one –"

"That's not fair, I told you that one, that doesn't count."

"And for another, he only goes to Galaxy meetings to be with you, not because he cares about writing at all, and also he's conceited."

"No, you don't know him. He is actually very insecure."

"Give me a break."

"He is. He has a lot of family problems."

"Like what?"

"Well, his parents fight a lot –"

"Big deal, at least they're not divorced."

"Yeah but his father puts a lot of pressure on him to do well in school, I mean like if he doesn't get an A in AP Physics they might not let him go to the senior prom –"

"And why do you think he tells you stuff like that?"

"What do you mean, *why*. We tell each other everything."

"Anyhow, his parents fighting doesn't give him a

right to act like an asshole."

"He doesn't act like an asshole, what are you talking about."

"He's just a dork. Everybody knows it."

"Everybody who?"

"Everybody."

"Josh, you do not know everybody."

"Yes I do."

"I mean I admit sometimes he can be a little obnoxious –"

"Sometimes?"

"Okay, a lot of the time, but he –"

"He must be great in bed."

"Shut up, Josh."

"Well is he?"

"Shut up."

"Because I figure he has no other good qualities so –"

"Josh, don't be a pain."

"So it must be sex."

"We've only been going out a year."

"So? A year is a long time."

"Not long enough for me. You know I would tell you if we were. I have no secrets. Yeesh! Don't worry, I'm still a virgin. So why are you acting like this?"

"Acting like what? This is my regular self."

"No it isn't."

"Okay, okay, I'm sorry."

"Look, I have to do my math."

"Don't be mad."

"No, I really have to go."

"Fine."

"So, bye."

"Bye."

§   §   §

Josh, Wanda, and I play cards at Josh's house, eating leftover matzo meal pancakes. The jungle pattern on the basement wallpaper is getting on my nerves. Josh and Wanda are playing gin rummy; I have winners. Wanda beats Josh by a mile, so I take his place on the couch and he sits on the washing machine playing "Southern Cross" on the guitar.

"Don't you know any other songs?"

"I can play 'Bad to the Bone' – would you prefer that?"

"NO," we yell, throwing the cards at him. The jack of diamonds gets stuck behind the dryer and we have to spend half an hour trying to get it out.

§   §   §

From the margin of my math class notebook:

Math class is even more boring than usual agh!

If Josh likes either of us, it is definitely me. This is flattering but makes me a little nervous. I like things the way they are. I don't want anything to change. If one of us fell in love with another of us that would ruin everything. Like right now when we get together and rent a movie we all sit on the couch on top of each other like a pile of hamsters at the pet store but if there was actual romance between any two of us we couldn't do that anymore, you know? Why do I talk to you like you have an opinion? You are only a notebook.

§   §   §

"What are we doing tonight?"

"I don't know, what do you want to do?"

"What is there to do?"

"We could go to the movies."

"I have no money."

"We could rent."

"Only if we decide what we're renting first."

"Yeah, Josh always takes too long at the video store."

"That's because I don't want to waste the night watching something lame."

"We could go to the playground," says Wanda, "And eat cookies."

"What kind of cookies?"

"Whatever kind you want, Simon."

"That's okay with me."

"What if it rains?"

"Then we'll rent a movie."

"What movie?"

"Why don't you wait until it rains," says Wanda,

"And then we'll decide what movie."

"I want Mallomars."

"That is not a movie."

"No, that is a cookie."

"I'm glad we've got that sorted out."

"I need a ride."

"Who's going to drive?"

"Well I'm sick of always driving," says Ray.

"But you're the only one with a car!"

"What if I drive your car?"

"Okay, Simon, but no swerving in any circular driveways if you don't mind."

"Should he pick us up at your house or my house?" I say to Wanda.

"Your house," says Wanda, "Because I have to drop off your long underwear."

"Did you hear that Ray? Pick us up at my house."

"How could I not hear that, Dora, you're screaming right in my ear."

"It's not my fault I have such a loud voice."

"But you don't have to use it all the time."

"How else could I talk to you?"

§   §   §

```
wghat is the problem of writing?
the problem of wrting is trying to say everything
in a finite space.\
no the problem of wirting is when you cant. I
mean can't.
```

I thenk the problem of wreting is that thaere
are too many rules and thay are all stuped.
for people such as ourselves in high school,
the problem of writing is that we wouldrather
not.
Yeah. boycott the scroll!
i'm addicted to the scroll.
the scroll is my lefe.
The problem of writing (if w e can get back
to the subject and you all can stop these
shenanigans!) is that we have to use words,
and there are only so many wo rds, and each
person has his or her own com plete language
that no one esle speaks.
what?
I don;'t understand
hahha very funny
what?

§   §   §

Ray speaks:

    I don't see what the big deal is. They were friends,
now they aren't. That happens to people all the time. You
just get sick of someone. You need to branch out, meet other
people. Yes, they did yell at each other once in a while,
usually over some really ridiculous philosophical issue
that didn't matter at all, but I think they just drifted apart,
you know? There was no big explosion or anything.

I have to say, whatever happened between them, it's a shame. They were such good friends, and they anchored the whole Galaxy crowd. I know about the shit that goes on at other schools, and I'm so glad we had each other. I mean, at my old school before this one I got so much more crap about the color of my skin, people calling me "oreo cookie," black on the outside and white on the inside – it sucked.

The divisions at Brighton aren't about color or religion, they are about what kind of sweater you wear. And we mostly stayed out of that, hanging out in the Galaxy room all the time. Dora and Wanda just didn't allow that stuff. Their hearts were in the right place, and I am going to miss them.

§   §   §

On Tuesdays after school I take the bus into the city to go to my voice lesson at the Eastman School of Music. I think of it as my howling lesson – controlled howling – a release of emotion. After all, emotion is all I am full of all week long; on Tuesday I allow it to pour out of me like lava.

Scales, art songs, jazz, the siren wails of warm-ups. I don't need the moon to howl; I barely need the piano – I control my yelling into music, and people applaud.

"You keep forgetting to breathe," says my voice instructor. "If you would just remember to breathe more, you might be a real diva."

I try to remember, really, I try, but I get so excited,

looking forward to the high A that is coming, or the rhythmic surprise, and then I have no air.

§ § §

From my English class notebook:

Going To the Galaxy Room

In the galaxy room there are pathways
you follow to find out what you want to know
imagine – somewhere in all these books
or on the face of the typewriter or in parentheses
at the back of the magazine there is
the perfect sentence, the answer to your question,
the words all around you like
the tornado in the Wizard of Oz never
go home Dorothy, Dorothy never land
language can be your bed, the
beautiful wonder of all possible poems

§ § §

"What is he *doing*?" I whisper to Wanda in a corner of the Galaxy room.
"Brunheubering."
"But *why?*"
"Maybe he has nothing to say."
"How can anyone have nothing to say?" I ask, since I always have something to say. In fact I have too much to

say. It's like when I was eleven years old in my Dorothy Hamill haircut (which later became known as the Princess Di haircut and then ceased to exist as a possible haircut at all), and I used to watch the ice skating on TV and think that if I had the whole ice rink to myself and no one in the way I could do those figure eights and jumps and twists too – similarly, I think, I am always in search of the high school equivalent of Siberia. If only I could be in a place where no one could hear me or see me, and I wouldn't bother anyone, I could sing my head off, really let everything that is in me out and it would come out *right*.

Another idea I had when I was eleven was that I had an inner perfect self. My fourth grade notebook contains this quote: "Inside of me, there is a much better girl, who is quiet and pretty and unaware, smart but not too smart." In fourth grade, apparently, quietness was attached to prettiness in a very clear logic. Pretty girls did not run around yelling and screaming and bugging everyone. Therefore being quiet and behaving yourself made you prettier.

Unfortunately the outer me could never quiet herself down enough to let this imaginary inner perfect self show. In fourth grade I was sure that this other self existed, that I only had to get to it. Now I am so much older and wiser; I know I can't be any quieter than I am, which is not quiet at all, and it's already such a strain.

What is Bill Brunheuber thinking at this very moment? Who knows. He does not speak or even type on the scroll.

§　§　§

Other kids in Galaxy start putting quotes on the Galaxy room door, but the Wandora Unit says we should be the only ones taping cards up there. We agree that our taste is better than other people's. So we make a Rule: only one index card allowed per day. And we mostly are the only ones who care enough to get up early and be the first to stick the card up there in the morning.

Certain Galaxy members seem to think Madonna lyrics count as poetry; Wanda and I put a quick stop to that. ("Okay, it's poetry if we go along with the idea that anything you call poetry can be poetry, but it's *bad* poetry.")

Josh and Simon get mad because they want to put up a quote from *The Blues Brothers* ("One prophylactic, soiled") but I tell them no one will get the reference and Wanda says the whole office could get in trouble for being obscene, which could be true.

Josh and Simon think we think we own the world. I guess we do think that. We think it so much we start making more rules:

No lunch trays in the office. No more than three non-Galaxy members in the office at a time. No jumping on the couch. No ethnic jokes. No poems with small i's unless they are by e.e. cummings. No copying homework, no badmouthing of Ms. Green, no whining, and no, absolutely no stupid boy bands on the radio.

We tape these rules to the walls of the Galaxy room

and point to them when there is a dispute. When someone disputes the rules themselves, we point to a sign that says **Dora and Wanda have the right to kick anyone out of the office who disputes the rules.**

We are becoming tyrants, and I can't seem to do anything about it. The Wandora Unit is like a blockade in Parcheesi; there we are with our twin heads and no one can get past us. Not even ourselves.

§   §   §

"I am Oz, the Great and Terrible," intones the wizard from the television in Wanda's den. I recite the next line along with Judy Garland:

"I am Dorothy, the small and meek."

"Why do you always have to say that?" asks Simon, cutting in on the scarecrow's line. "You say it every year."

"I don't know, I just like the rhythm of it."

"Because you're not meek at all."

"Yeah," agrees Josh, "In fact you have a pretty big mouth."

"I am *aware* of that, you heartless fiend!"

"Would you guys be quiet, please?" says Ray, "The lion is about to jump through the glass."

"I hate this part."

Wanda does not say a word. She is strangely characterless. She watches the movie in a detached fashion, hardly paying attention, because she is afraid she's pregnant. But I don't find that out until later night when everyone else has gone home.

The next day, I borrow a car and we drive to East Henrietta to buy a pregnancy test ("You want the one with the stick or the one with the cup?" "I think I'm going to faint") and then administer it in my bathroom. It comes out light pink.

"What does pink mean?"

"Pink is bad."

"Oh, please tell me you're kidding, please tell me you're joking, this is the worst joke in the world Dora –"

"Wait! It's always pink! The question is, where is it pink! Which section?"

"I don't know. You look at it. I'm going to start crying soon."

"Don't cry. That's the test side. That's supposed to be pink. You're fine! You're not pregnant!"

"Hurray hurray hurray hurray!"

We dance around the room hugging.

"Let's call Norris."

"I didn't tell Norris."

"What do you mean you didn't tell Norris? You told me and not Norris?"

"Well, of course."

"And if you'd been pregnant, would you have named me as the father?"

"But I'm not pregnant. I'm not pregnant! I think I'll paint my bedroom walls this beautiful shade of pink."

"So you're not going to tell him?"

"I don't think so. It would just upset him."

"But you *should* upset him! You were upset!"

"He couldn't take it. He'd be a nervous wreck."

"Good! Let him be a little nervous. Besides, it's all over now."

"So why bother him?"

"I can't believe you told me and not Norris."

"I tell you everything, dummy. How could I not tell you?"

§   §   §

Life is serious but art is fun!

– clown in John Irving's
The Hotel New Hampshire

§   §   §

Last night, I caught a glimpse of my soul as I was drifting off to sleep. It is shaped like a cantaloupe, a rindless orange melon in the center of my body. In this same way, on other nights, I have seen music (yellow bands of light moving across a staff) and also the physical apparition of a book I was reading (it appeared as a set of three-dimensional interlocking beige blocks).

It seems that Wanda's soul is a pine tree, that Ernie's is a brown horse, that Josh's is a melting star. Simon's looks like a lizard; Ray's is a red plastic pail full of beach sand. Norris does not have a soul.

The visions come quickly once activated: Yvonne Pie's soul is greasy; Laurie Leach's soul is a white mouse fluffed up with a blow dryer; Karen's is an empty blackboard; Tom's is a lazy-boy chair permanently stuck in the back position; Melissa's is a field of daisies. Suzie's is a hot pink toothbrush. Monica's is a sailboat frozen in ice, Talya's is a feathered hat, and Bill Brunheuber's is a hula hoop. Ms. Green's soul is a floating high school.

Frank O'Hara's soul is cherry ice cream being thrown out of a helicopter!

§   §   §

Chapter VI: In Which, On Our Way to School at 7:01 in the Morning, Wanda and I Discuss Endings in Literature:

"You know what I hate?" I ask.

"No, what?"

"I hate when a movie ends with a line of dialog from the beginning of the movie."

"I hate that too," says Wanda, "And the same thing in books. They're trying to delude the audience into believing that life makes sense and goes in a circle."

"But it doesn't."

"Exactly."

"You can interpret your life to be that if you want, though – like Shakespeare dying on his birthday."

"I plan to die on your birthday."

"Okay, that'll work, and I'll die on yours."

"Who will die first?"

"This is morbid."

"Good."

"I think you should die first."

"Hey!"

"Then I'll weep and wail and publish our memoirs."

"The Wandora Memoirs."

"Will anyone read them?"

"Of course they will!"

§　§　§

From my journal:

Fri., really late at night like it's probably Sat. by now

if you don't mind, ol' journal ol' pal, there are certain sections of you I'd just rather not read again, okay? I'm going to glue some pages closed so I can't even accidentally turn to them. Some poems are so horribly written that I don't even want to revise them. I just want to rip them out. But what if later I change my mind? So I'll just glue them shut. Also there are certain subjects that make me feel sick inside and I would just rather not give them any more thought than I already have. So I'm sorry if I'm hurting your feelings journal my dear but I just think my feelings are more important than yours.

§　§　§

"Why do you love Norris?"

"Because he is good, and cute, and smart, and

because he loves me. Why do you love Ernie?"

"Because I can't help it."

§   §   §

Practically all our friends are writers, so we have to edit their poems. That's our job! We are editors of Galaxy; it is our job to edit. But lately it seems like we are so intoxicated with power that we are stomping all over our friends' stories and poems just because we can. It is amazing that we are forgiven.

§   §   §

Wanda and Josh and I sit on the washer and dryer in Josh's basement while he puts in load after load of laundry. We are talking about religion and death and desire. "Female desire," says Wanda, "is for love, not sex."

"No," I say, "*our* desire is for love, not sex."

"Well, yeah, that's what I mean."

"I mean we hardly even talk to other girls."

"That's probably true."

Josh can hardly get a word in edgewise. "I had a dream about you two," he says in a pause, "we were..."

"I mean we all know, if the world were ending, you and I would be screaming for love, but maybe some people would, like, just grab the nearest stranger and start, you know, having sex."

I try to lower my voice so I won't wake Josh's parents, but it is nearly impossible for me to talk quietly about something so important. The washer and dryer jiggle beneath the three of us as we talk into the early hours of the morning.

My mother thinks I am sleeping at Wanda's. Wanda's parents think she is sleeping at my house. Josh eventually falls asleep curled up by the dryer, but Wanda and I do not sleep at all.

§   §   §

Last summer, Wanda and I went to her family's place in New Hampshire. We spent most days lying on a raft in the lake. To get there we had to carry our books over our heads, hands lifted high above the water, swimming by kicking our feet only. I was reading *Setting Free the Bears* by John Irving. Wanda was reading *Their Eyes Were Watching God* by Zora Neale Hurston. The sun was hot. We slept at Wanda's family's summer house, a run-down cabin that used to be a camp shelter. Late in the evenings, we ate chef's salad and french bread for dinner. Sometimes we drove into town to go to the movies.

Wanda's bathing suit was red. Mine was black. That was pretty much the only way to tell us apart.

§   §   §

"Ernie! Where are we going to go for dinner before the prom?"

"Why do I have to decide?"

"Well you don't, but you have to suggest."

"Well, how expensive should it be?"

"Very, very expensive. I don't know! How much money can you spend?"

"I can't spend very much."

"Me neither."

"What color should the corsage be? Should it match your dress?"

"I don't know these things. Do I really have to wear high heels?"

"I don't care if you wear them or not."

"Then I'm not wearing them."

"My father will take thousands of pictures."

"The band is going to suck and I will be wearing the only green dress."

"I am going to have the best looking date."

"No, I am."

"Whose car should we take?"

"Your dad's car is cooler than my mom's."

"Dora, let's face it, the whole thing is going to be lame."

"Yes, but in a fun way."

"I need black socks."

"Let's just stay home."

"Yeah, it's not like it's the prom or anything."

"Wanda is going to wear gloves, and Norris is going to wear a top hat."

"How nice of Norris to deign to go to the prom. Is Josh going?"

"You know Josh doesn't have a date."

"Well, if he gets a date."

"He won't get a date unless he asks someone, which he won't."

"I know, let's dye our hair some strange color the day before."

"Oh, that's romantic."

"Dora, how long have we been together?"

"Like, a year and a half – you have to ask?"

"No, I mean just now."

"Oh, almost three mods."

"I'm late"

"Bye"

(kiss)

"Bye"

§　§　§

At four o'clock in the afternoon, the Wandora Unit is sitting on the top row of the bleachers at a track meet, waiting for the boys' 800 meter, Simon's event. The sun is getting lower. The Wandora Unit can see Simon shucking off his Brighton Track sweatpants and stretching his calves.

"Aren't we lucky we have such a cute friend?" I say.

Wanda replies, "It's not luck, we deserve it. We're cute too."

"Do you think we'll ever be old and ugly?"

"No way, and even if we are, we'll still have each other. We'll be toothless old ladies in rocking chairs on the front porch, but we'll still be best friends and smarter than everybody."

"You know, I can't imagine anything you might do that would make us stop being friends."

"Yeah, I mean say you murdered Simon in a fit of insanity – I'd be pretty upset, but I'd still visit you in jail."

"Me too. Let's not tell Simon."

"No, we better not."

I poke Wanda's knee. Wanda gives my shoulder an affectionate shove.

"You know what I think?" asks Wanda. "I think everyone else wishes they were us."

"Yeah."

"Because anyone who knew us would want to be like this."

§   §   §

Sometimes I think all times are pretty much the same. You can look at things from different directions and they will look different but they are not. My childhood was happy, unhappy, just there … my future is seething with light, is a valley of gloom, is a block of marble with something mysterious inside. Some composer once said that music is for the time before we were born. Writing may also be for a time different than this, a time you can't point to, when I and all the people I have ever loved exist as electrons circling the same tiny tiny thing and there are no words.

Other times it seems like there are enormous gaps

between one moment and the next, so wide and deep I could fall in and never climb out. Am I the same person I was this whole year? Will I be a totally new person some day? I wonder what will happen to Wanda and me. Will we always be friends, as we promise each other? Will we find substitutes for each other in college, people worthy of our secrets? Sometimes I feel like she is getting away from me, or I am getting away from her. I don't know if I'm escaping or being abandoned.

§　§　§

"Has anyone ever noticed this place has no windows?"

"The newspaper office has windows."

"So does the yearbook office."

"We must have a window."

"We deserve a window."

"We must have poetic justice."

"Let's make a window."

"Pass the chainsaw."

"But there's no outside out there."

"Huh?"

"It's a classroom on this side, the hall on that side, what's on this side?"

"The library, duh"

"Oh yeah and on this side, a janitor's closet."

"Well, let's paint a window."

"With a view of Paris!"

"Paris, schmaris."

"Okay, what should it be then?"

"Oz?"

"The hills of Switzerland?"

"No it should be a window into another office just like this one."

"And in that room, another window..."

"Yes!"

"Until finally, very small in the very last window, a summer's day."

"Ray, you are a genius."

§   §   §

Josh breaks his collarbone riding on the back bumper of Simon's car as Simon backs out of Ray's driveway. It is snowing, and icy, and Simon does not know Josh is there until he falls off. Ray's mother is a doctor and insists that Josh go to the emergency room because something is definitely not right with Josh's back or arm, in fact something is broken, in fact it's his collarbone.

I ride in the backseat as Ray drives a trying-not-to-cry Josh to the hospital. Simon, wracked with guilt (although it's hardly his fault) drives behind us with Wanda. Every bump the car goes over, Josh flinches, and a tiny tear lurches out of one of his eyes – first the left, then the right, then the left again, and so on. I am almost mesmerized by this, but to entertain Josh and make him stop thinking about it, I tell the Yellow Ribbon story.

There once was a lady who always wore a

yellow ribbon around her neck. So one day she met a man who fell in love with her mainly because he found the yellow ribbon thing so intriguing. "Why do you wear that yellow ribbon all the time" he asked her, but she wouldn't say. So they courted for a long time and finally he asked her to marry him. When the lady said yes, he said, "So now will you tell me why you wear that yellow ribbon?" "No," she said, "But I will tell you on our wedding night." So they got married a year after that, and on their wedding night the man was all excited to find out, and he asked her again, and she said, "Oh honey you've waited so long you can wait a little longer. I will tell you after we have been married for five years." But after five years she said the same thing again, this time she said she would tell him on their twenty-fifth wedding anniversary. But when their twenty-fifth anniversary rolled around, she told him to wait until their fiftieth: "You've waited so long, you can wait a little longer." But on their fiftieth anniversary she became very ill and had to lie in bed all the time. Her husband, who loved her very much by this time, stayed by her and comforted her and stuff, and a year or two went by like that. Finally the doctor said she would probably die that night. So the husband says to the lady, "I love you so much," blah blah blah, "But will you please, please tell me why you wear that yellow ribbon around your neck now?" So the lady untied the yellow ribbon from around her neck, and her head fell off.

Josh does not like this story; he does not think it is funny, but stupid. "That was a very stupid story," he says to me groggily in the parking lot, after having his collarbone reset in the hospital.

"Would you like to hear it again for the way home?"

"Please ride in the other car with Wanda and Simon. Tell the story to them."

"I already told them while we were waiting for you in the horrible emergency room waiting room."

"Did they like it?"

A chorus of nos, and it is one o'clock in the morning, still snowing, we all get in our cars and go home. The streets of Rochester are practically empty. There will be no chocolate chip pancakes at Perkins tonight.

§   §   §

It is an unbearably beautiful day. Wanda and I are so happy we can hardly stand ourselves.

In the morning on the way to school the sky is lavender as stationery, that almost-rain color of clouds, and the world is poignant and profound, and every word we say to each other is enveloped in our expecta of the rain to come.

At school the windows are pelted with it, rain interrupting the classes on the north side of the building with its loudness.

By the last mod, the rain whisks itself away. All five of us – me, Wanda, Josh, Simon, and Ray – meet at the door to the Galaxy room, buy donuts and french fries in the cafeteria, and devour them under the climbing thing on the elementary school playground. We revel in the revoltingness of what we're eating, me yammering non-stop, the air wet and full around us.

Our voices (especially mine) carry over the football field, through neighborhoods, past Niagara Falls, on beyond zebra; the day is perfect, the salt and chocolate divine, Wanda and I walk home practically holding hands with happiness. Nothing happened today besides the weather, but we don't care.

§   §   §

"No, not really," say Wanda and I, on being asked if we mind being called the Wandora Unit.

"Actually, we like it." "We like it."

We speak simultaneously, like Siamese twins in a bad movie. But I detect a difference in the tone of the way we answer. Wanda is simply proud; I am defiant. I know we are being insulted.

§   §   §

From my journal:

I've changed my mind again. Now I think Wanda was right after all. I am jealous of her. It pisses me off that she has all these poems written about her and I have none. Norris writes her such romantic poems! He is so much more boyfriendy than Ernie is. No one ever buys me roses of any color. Or jewelry. Well, I don't like jewelry. But I wouldn't mind chocolates. I guess I just don't inspire presents. Or it could have to do with the fact that Ernie doesn't ever have any money. Still. I have to try to be less this way. I have to try to be more demure.

§   §   §

"You know what's wrong with Bill Brunheuber?" I ask, looking forward to telling the answer.

"What *isn't* wrong with him? Well, he's cute, but besides that."

"He looks at you like he's reading a teleprompter across your chest."

"Yeah! That's true! He's always looking slightly below your eyes, kind of like this —"

"Stop it! That's creepy!"

"Maybe he is looking at our breasts!"

"But he does it to guys also — maybe he thinks we all have words there for him to say to us?"

"Too bad we don't — we could script him."

"He needs a script. He never speaks. Is he shy?"

"No, he has nothing to say," says Wanda, who

automatically knows this, apparently.

"But what is he thinking about?"

"Nothing, I guess. I mean if he was thinking, he'd have to talk, right? I mean talking is for cleaning out our brains, so we can have more thoughts."

"I think that's only for you and me. Other people don't need to express their thoughts to have them."

"I don't believe that."

"I guess I don't either, really."

§   §   §

This morning I have an argument with Wanda in the shower. No, of course Wanda is not in the shower! She is in her own house, in her own shower probably. But I yell at her in my head, which isn't really fair, because she can't fight back.

The hot water starts to run out, but I keep going. That poem in French should not be in the magazine. Just because Wanda speaks French doesn't mean everybody else can. If the poem were in Spanish Wanda would want a translation and it's just, well, it's, it's *snobbish* and besides the poem isn't all that great *anyway* and why can't I say this to Wanda in person, at school, in the Galaxy room?

This is because the two of us have made a pact not to disagree in public. Usually this is easy since we usually agree. But sometimes Wanda can be so domineering. Mentally, I lie down in the tub to drown, since it is my own fault. I am afraid to incur the wrath of Wanda. Uncertain as to what the origin of Wanda's authority may be, it is so impenetrable a power that no one has ever dared challenge it. Because Wanda believes she is right, what she thinks becomes right. No one ever tells her this is the reason for her loneliness.

Except me in the bathroom, the water pouring down, across the street and soundlessly. Wanda might say such hurtful things in return, things that I have seen sitting just beneath her eyes in other arguments. It's ridiculous! Why am I afraid of my best friend?

§   §   §

RING

"You know what's really stupid about this Be Yourself moral?"

"What, Dora, is really stupid about the Be Yourself moral."

"Well it's so stupid because they're acting like you have a choice! I mean who else could you be? If you're a total phony fake person then that's exactly what you are, and you shouldn't kid yourself that there's a secret you that is different!"

"My, you're in a ranting and raving mood today. Something happen?"

"No, not at all. I've just been thinking about it."

"You're right, you know, like I bet Heather Smith goes to bed every night thinking that she is a really a very nice person, and it's just peer pressure that makes her act like such a snob."

"Josh, you understand. Should I ride over?"

"Yep."

§ § §

"Orange whip? Orange whip? Three orange whips."

On Friday night the five of us rent *The Blues Brothers* again. Ray delivers commentary on the TV version vs. the original: "On TV Aretha says shi-oot instead of shit." "I don't think they can say prophylactic on television, and they definitely can't talk about used prophylactics..."

"Ray, can you shut up, please? I'm trying to watch a movie here."

"Yeah, what she said."

"It's not like you don't know what's going to happen and I'm ruining the suspense."

"When are they going to drive through the mall? I love it when they drive through the mall."

We are in Simon's basement. Girl Scout cookies abound.

§ § §

Wanda speaks:

I'd say our friendship went through a progression like a bell curve. I think there was a problem with jealousy, and maybe it was on both sides. And sometimes we had very stupid arguments. The flowers argument, for example. Before Dora and I knew each other, I doubt either of us gave any thought to a philosophy of flowers. But last summer when we walked around in the woods in New Hampshire and in the garden behind my family's summer house, we were just thrilled by everything – the beautiful roses and snapdragons and things that my mother planted, and also the dandelions, daisies, pansies, things like that. We were, you know, *dazzled*, not giving much thought to it, just enjoying them together, all the flowers equally, nudging each other occasionally on our walks together to point out each new thing. I suppose we thought of ourselves as somehow privileged – after all, not everyone gets to spend a morning just walking and looking at flowers. Then later, when we talked about it, we had this long, involved *debate* about the flowers, because when I mentioned I preferred garden flowers – cut flowers are so delicate, they have an aesthetic grace, an elegance, you know? – Dora got all mad for some reason, and said she liked the weeds better, because no one planted them, they just grew. Because they were accidental. It was all quite odd, really, and I must confess I have never understood why it became such an argument.

§ § §

While Norris is in France for spring break, Wanda mopes around pretending she doesn't care. "I'm trying my best not to mind that he's away," she tells me, "But I think it's like in the cartoons, when they tiptoe around in the snow so they won't start an avalanche down the mountain."

"But avalanches start for no reason."

"Don't remind me."

§　§　§

"I think #70 is about drugs."

"Well, duh, of course it is. It's really depressing, too."

"Why is his coat bloody?"

"Or her coat."

"Why is *the* coat bloody?"

"It isn't, that's just a drug fantasy."

"Well, excuse me, I guess I don't know enough about drug fantasies."

"I like the line about the prism bloom. That's really nice."

"I like the fact that this poem is not about love."

§　§　§

In AP English Wanda, Simon, and I sit together in a row. We are in a paradise of desks; we raise our hands up in a perfect line of hands, Wanda's, then mine, then Simon's, to every question.

Ms. Green tries to convince the class in three foot tall letters on the board that CREON KNEW HE WAS WRONG. The Wandora Unit thinks of itself as Antigone. We plan to be Antigone forever in the face of the poemless world – we will not let Nicole Turner copy our homework – we will not tie our pinneys in gym class – we will not stand by while Nathan Phelps gets beaten up at the bus stop – we will not sell the chocolates. We will always tell the truth. At Galaxy meetings we will never divulge, nor even hint, who wrote the poems being discussed. We will not go to church, not say the Pledge to the Flag in homeroom, not stamp our feet at the stupid pep rally. We will not think of ourselves as part of any institutionalized group! (We do not think of Galaxy as an institutionalized group.) We will be responsible for the consequences of our actions! We will love Ms. Green long after she forgets us and we are old and we still don't think Creon knew he was wrong but we agree that he *was* wrong and Antigone was right and Ms. Green still affects us from the past.

§   §   §

From my journal:

I don't care if Norris was in Paris, wherever he was, it's disgusting! Even if it was only a kiss (which I DOUBT), he cheated. I told Wanda I wanted to cut off his feet for doing this to her how could he do this to her? but she's acting like she doesn't even mind that he dumped her, like she wanted to break up with him anyway, which is a total falsehood. when I say that about cutting off his feet in revenge Wanda laughs this makes her feel better I am cheering her up I want her to be happy. but I guess I embarrassed her by saying that she was better off without him I guess I said it too loud she told me to lower my voice and I thanked her for telling me!

§ § §

I've always been especially drawn to books about rooms: John Fowles's *Mantissa*; Marguerite Duras's *The Malady of Death*; Nabokov's *Invitation to a Beheading*.

As you go deeper into each of these stories, the room takes on new proportions. It is a room, a house, a prison cell, an insane asylum, a body, a family, a brain. Everything happens in the room, and people only dream of leaving. Even when they dream, they can only dream about the room.

§ § §

Wanda wants nothing more than to go to Harvard, where her parents went. She is so sure she will be happy there. She's already all set – she applied early and got in. The day that letter came she was so happy – so *relieved*. If she hadn't gotten accepted, her parents probably would have disowned her, or that's the way they act. Like Harvard is where she *belongs*, and nowhere else will do. Like there's only one right place for her.

I applied to five colleges, all small, and all near big cities. Swarthmore gave me a good scholarship so that's where I'm going. I'll be able to eat falafel any time I want and see art movies and the library will have every book I can think to look up! I'm going to read Stevie Smith and Frank O'Hara and study Duchamp's "The Large Glass" at the Philadelphia Museum of Art. And the boys there will be different. They'll wear big black shoes and like bands

I've never heard of. I'll work on a literary magazine at Swarthmore, probably, but I'll try not to let it permeate my life the way Galaxy has.

Ernie doesn't know what the hell he is doing. He wanted to apply to just the places where I applied! I told him that's a dumb way to make decisions, just to follow your girlfriend. He might take a year off and work for his uncle in New York.

Everyone is moving away – we're all going to be in different places next year. Josh is going to an international program at Georgetown. Simon is going to Cornell. Ray is going to art school in North Carolina. They all seem so sure of themselves. I feel like I'm doing my best to stay where I am and not slip backward, and they are all flying off to different people, across oceans, into other languages.

§   §   §

On Friday afternoon, Wanda calls me. "What are we doing tonight?"

"Have you talked to Simon or anybody?"

"Ray said we can't go to his house."

"I'll call Josh and you call Simon. Then call me back. Or should I call you back?"

"You call me back because you'll be on the phone longer," says Wanda.

"Hi, Josh?" "Yeah." "So who won in tennis golf?" "I trounced him	"Hello, may I speak to Simon?" "Simon! Telephone! I think it's

with two under par for the whole course." "How do you know what's par when you make up the course as you go along? I bet you decide what's par after you take your turn and then Simon has to try to keep up." "No, smartypants, we decide the final par in advance and then we decide the holes." "Well excuuuuse me. I didn't realize it was as complicated as Kapcki Mapcki." "At least the rules stay the same. Why is Kapcki Mapcki called that anyway?" "Because of the poster of Karl Marx in the Galaxy room that Norris put up." "He would." "Anyhow it's got Karl Marx's name on the bottom in Cyrillic, and Ernie or Ray or somebody said one day 'who's Kapcki Mapcki' and then somebody used the poster as a target in

Dora but it could be Wanda." "Hi, Dora?" "No, it's Wanda." "Good, because Dora always blasts me with her voice and I have to hold the phone two feet away from my ear." "So what are we doing tonight?" "Didn't Ray call you?" "No, but I've been on the phone with Dora." "Well you're welcome to come over here and watch *Spinal Tap* if you want." "Cool." "Ray said he would pick you guys up and then you can go to Wegmans and get the movie on the way to my house."

"Hi Wanda?" "Ray! How nice of you to offer to pick us up!" "My psychic powers tell me that you have been on the phone with Simon."

the game..." "So Kapcki Mapcki is named after a communist." "Got a problem with that?" "No, no, you know I'm a communist myself." "Yeah, me too. So what are we doing tonight?"

"Magic. Amazing." "I'll pick you up in between your houses like usual at about 7:30."

§ § §

At play rehearsal, I can yowl and caterwaul all I want. "Goodbye, goodbye, goodbye," I sing to Mr. Vandergelder at the top of my lungs. At rehearsal, I am fully self-actualized. You're *supposed* to talk loudly on stage. It's called projecting. "Boy, that girl can project," I heard the stage manager whisper to the director. "That's why we chose her," the director said. "She has no acting experience, but at least we can hear her. And she sure can sing." I take this as a compliment. Acting is just pretending, not real. Singing is REAL.

Of the five of us, only Josh is in the musical. The others have track or aren't interested. Wanda is not interested. Well, she tried out, but when she only got in the chorus, she decided she wasn't interested. Too bad, because it would have been fun to hang out at rehearsal. Anyhow, every time Josh sings "Well, well, hello, Dolly," I almost crack up on stage. After rehearsal, digging into chocolate chip pancakes at Perkins (Open 24 Hours), I tell Josh that if Louis Armstrong had been a white suburban nerd, he would have been just like Josh. This makes Josh very proud.

§   §   §

"#71 makes no sense. 'Filmature' is not a word, and neither is 'Linguinium.'"

"Well, it says words are inconstant."

"I don't understand this."

"Maybe you're not supposed to understand it."

"What's the point of writing poetry for no one to understand?"

"Ask Ezra Pound. Half of those cantos he wrote aren't even in English!"

"I like the "Floating: above our heads" part because it's like a dictionary definition of the dictionary."

"Oooo, self referential."

"The more self referential the better."

"This is a sentence, yeah, yeah."

§   §   §

A month after graduation, while taking a lunch break from my summer job, I am suddenly overwhelmed for no reason with the thought of Wanda.

I'm sitting at a small table at Aladdin's on Monroe Avenue, most of the room empty. If Wanda were here with me, I think, lunch would take on grand philosophical meaning, even if it was false meaning, and it would be much more exciting. Every lunch would be like that, and life would feel different. Uncertain as I feel about the slow demise of the Wandora Unit, at this moment I am struck with nostalgia for the intensity of the friendship.

As I leave the restaurant, I note that the frozen yogurt flavors of the day are Chocolate, Raspberry, and Swedish Vanilla. What is Swedish Vanilla? If Wanda were here, I think to myself, she would think that was funny. I consider calling Wanda to tell her about it, but dismiss the thought immediately. I can't call the Wanda I am thinking of, because that person does not exist.

PART III

Wanda and I are spinning around Wanda's living room. If you do it fast enough, and well enough, you feel dizzy and fall down, which is what we are trying to do.

We are wrecking the furniture. Barefoot, we stomp around the house and then wash our feet in the sink. Wanda's parents have gone on a trip, and the world belongs to the Wandora Unit.

We put up signs everywhere. On the cupboard: **Simon and Josh are coming – hide the potato chips!**; on the bathroom door: **Maxi-Pads are for Wimps**; on the living room wall: **Don't Drink: Spin!** For dinner we cook frozen ravioli and do not have a salad. Wanda sets the table weirdly. I make chocolate egg creams. We are on the phone the *entire time*.

The jubilation of music is incredible: we play the Talking Heads, the Eurythmics, a collection of Norwegian folk songs which sets us to a new round of spinning. We find a Sesame Street disco recording and dance like John Travolta in *Saturday Night Fever* as if we invented that joke, laughing uproariously.

When Wanda's parents call to check on us, we shut everything down, even our faces, and manage not to giggle but to sound as serious and responsible as we need to be.

That night we stay up until three in the morning and sleep on the floor, spun out, teeth unbrushed, refrigerator humming, windows open, clocks unplugged.

Chapter CCXXVI: In Which Wanda and I Go to the Printer's:

"We want plenty of white space."

"White space is what we want."

"So, what you girls are saying is, you want lots of white space. Well you realize that means less text."

"That's okay."

"We're elitists about text, populists about white space."

"Then white space is what you shall have. Finally, some teenagers with taste in graphics!"

"Also, we want wingdings on the sides of the numbers."

"And we want really cool fonts."

"Do you have any really cool fonts?"

"Really cool, I don't know, but I have many volumes of fonts for you to look through. I'll go drink my coffee and you can look at all the fonts in all the books."

"Just don't forget the white space."

"Girls, there's white space all around us. How could I forget?"

§   §   §

Josh and I are driving around the streets of Rochester after play rehearsal. The city is as empty as the ghost town in that episode of *The Brady Bunch* where they get trapped in a jail cell and use a belt to get the keys. Josh plays the radio, methodically popping a tape in and out of the tape player to avoid the bad songs on 98 WPXY.

What do we talk about? We talk and talk, and drive and drive, but later I remember none of the conversation, just the dark streets ahead of us, buildings on each side, 11:00 at night, not wanting to go home, and the final car door slam in the suburbs.

§   §   §

"We shall now discuss poem #75, 'One Brief Moment.' Does anyone have any thoughts about this poem's meaning?"

"Birth."

"Death."

"No, no, this is like, when you come in the room, and you turn on the light, and the light doesn't go on because it's broken or the bulb is burnt out or something, and just for a second you're terrified! But then the light does go on after all. And that's all it's about! It's not about anything else!" splutters Gina.

"How would you know? You're not the poet."

"Actually, I am."

"Then you're not allowed to talk at all. Don't you know what a breach of rules it is to break the anonymity of poems at meeting?" says Wanda, outraged.

"But…" says Gina.

"Be quiet."

"But…" I say.

"The Wandora Unit has spoken," says Wanda, speaking for both of us. This never used to bother me.

§ § §

Chapter CXXV: In Which Ernie and I Have Sex For the First Time, and It Is a Disaster:

Ernie's parents are going out of town. O magical phrase! Where do they go? I don't know and Ernie doesn't care. We have been waiting for an opportunity like this.

The week before his parents leave, Ernie endeavors to acquire a condom. First he fakes sick to get into the nurse's office, where, rumor has it, a basket of condoms sits on a coffee table in the waiting area. But the fabled basket, while present, is empty, and a forlorn Ernie tells the nurse he suddenly feels better after all.

Kevin Sullivan, whose locker is next to Ernie's, is always offering to sell condoms to everybody; he is also a source for marijuana, fake IDs, and pornography. Kevin claims to have sex all the time ("Every night, man, every night"), but the condom Ernie surreptitiously buys from him on Wednesday afternoon is a Trojan in an orange wrapper. This means it is non-lubricated (the lubricated ones have blue wrappers), and I have heard that non-lubricated is no good (and also that "Ribbed for her pleasure" is meaningless) and so, finally, we decide to make a trek ourselves to get some at the drugstore.

On Thursday after school, Ernie and I get my mother's car ("Mom, can I borrow the car?" "Sure –

where're you going?" "To … the … um … Wegmans" "Can you pick up some frozen grape juice while you're at it?" "I guess so –") and drive twenty miles to a CVS out in East Henrietta where no one will know us. It is actually the same drugstore where Wanda and I bought her pregnancy test – I wonder if they remember me and think I'm some kind of deranged sex fiend!

There we buy a package of three lubricated Trojans, a chapstick, and a birthday card for Ray. On the way back we remember the frozen grape juice and we stop off at Wegmans and the line is really long and I try to come up with some story explaining why I have been gone two hours but my mother does not ask.

The next day, Ernie and I take Ernie's bus together after school. The bus driver does not recognize me and gives me a funny look. Ernie says I am his cousin. I say that is disgusting.

In Ernie's bedroom, we sit on the bed, Ernie's Tears for Fears album facing us from the shelf opposite. I can't help but remember Wanda's description of losing her virginity to Norris – "It was absolutely perfect," Wanda said, "he was very gentle," but she would not look at me when she said it, and she would not give details except to say it didn't hurt as much as she expected.

"Well!" I say brightly, and Ernie pounces on me, and we make out lying on the bed the same as usual, for what feels like an hour, like forever, because neither one of us wants to rush the other into what we know we are about to do. We are both terribly nervous, but trying to be brave.

Our clothes slowly move off our bodies onto the floor. Now I am utterly naked, a state I have achieved many times before but never with such purpose, and at the same time Ernie is also naked, which is not normally allowed – we normally trade off nakedness, to avoid mutual nudity and the danger that follows.

When Ernie tries to unwrap the condom it slips out of his fingers and falls behind the bed, and I reach for it, my arm searching beside the bed, and I get the condom and unwrap it and look at the thing, so plastic, so tender, so silly looking, I don't really know what to do with it; I have read the instructions on the box five times but I'm afraid of putting it on inside-out and hurting Ernie somehow, damaging his most precious, most mysterious part.

I make a face. Ernie responds with the same face. "We're morons!"

Ernie reads the box one more time and rolls the condom on himself.

Watching him, I am transfixed, remembering the first time I touched Ernie's penis. I'm pretty familiar with it by now, but the first time, I barely brushed it, both of us lying sideways on his bed after a Galaxy meeting one night, and suddenly there was white sticky stuff all over my stomach, and we were laughing and hugging, and Ernie kept saying "holy shit!"

I wish I could say that everything just flows naturally for us this first time we have sex, violins playing in the background, but that isn't the truth. It's a good thing Ernie's family is away for the entire weekend, because our first attempt is a failure, and so, half an hour later, is the second; but four hours later, sore, frustrated, feeling that there must be something wrong with us, we make a third and final try with the last condom ("I'm not driving all the way out to East Henrietta again" says Ernie) and something goes differently, goes *right*, and Ernie and I fall away from each other exhausted, happy, prideful, changed in our own minds. We were in love before this, and now we are still in love, but there is a difference. Maybe not in the first second after we get dressed, but there is a change in the way we love each other.

Sex feels like our own private knowledge, a new and worthwhile secret that both strengthens and harms the way we feel about each other. To be that close for some minutes and then not to be – to realize you can never not be alone, that even when you are in love you are still alone. It is sad; it is the best thing in the world.

§ § §

He could do this great trick with his drool, after he'd been running or playing soccer. He could spit like six inches of spit and the saliva would extend from his mouth down toward the floor and then he could pull it back up again. Like a yo-yo of drool. That impressed me.

Also, he brooded, he had this mysteriousness, as if he had terrible secrets, and I thought if I could penetrate, get him to tell me these secrets, then I would know something that I had never known before and that no one else knew and we would belong to each other forever in the deepest most hidden places of our souls. That's what I *thought*.

But it didn't turn out that way. It's like I just *decided* that Ernie told me everything, that he could not possibly lie to me, that we had some sort of all-transcending love that was bigger than the human body. I think people can imagine whole personalities and impose them on unsuspecting strangers and no one ever recovers from this.

I mean, yes, Ernie is in the deepest most hidden place of my soul. But does he belong there? Is that where he should be? Am I in his? If I could answer these questions I could call him up on the phone and say "Yes, Ernie, it is I, and I will not leave you this time if you will only please please take me back," or "Ernie, never think of me again, for our futures are unrelated." Blah! As if!

Wanda once told me she thinks girls eventually have to leave their best friends for boys, but I don't think she's an expert on the matter. And obviously, neither am I.

Ernie and I will always have each other's virginities, but the Galaxy room is really going to disappear. Soon there will be no evidence that we were ever here. In a way, I like that. But in another way, I hate it. I want to make something permanent. A monument to NOW.

§   §   §

February, melting snow – fire drill season. We've had four or five of them in the past week. Today, when the bells go off, Wanda and Josh and I end up on the same side of the building and so we go sit under the flagpole, our coats between us and the wet grass. Hundreds of people stream out of the doors and surround the school, but they are not interesting; they are like books on shelves in the sections of the library where you never go. Wanda and Josh and I are only interested in ourselves. Of course there is no fire, but it is unseasonably warm and the alarm keeps ringing and the fire trucks arrive and everyone is happy happy happy because we are losing more than a mod of class.

  After a few minutes, Ernie comes sweeping around the far side of the school and puts his warm hand on the back of my neck. A fire drill is like Mardi Gras – suddenly you can do whatever you want in a place where usually you can only do what you don't want. Some kids even get into cars and go home! Not us, though. We don't mind just sitting here, yanking up grass and throwing it at each other, using up class time outdoors.

§   §   §

From my journal:

Why does she have such a hard time saying she's sorry she never says it not the time I was in gym class with her and Sarah and they were mad at me and when we had to pick partners they picked each other never told me what they were mad about then there was the time with the socks. I don't know who threw first in the girls' locker room with its big mirror and lots of girls around and Wanda and I were so mad at each other we couldn't speak like always like up on the roof we read Romeo and Juliet showing off for the neighborhood such good friends everyone said they're so alike confusing us at school we were proud of that time with the socks we were so mad I throw a sock she throws one the other girls get out of the way we never hit or kicked I think some people would have liked to see us fight ("girlfighting") but we just threw socks. I am so angry I can only say "Oh" Wanda throws socks back at me sneakers too everything in the gym locker towels shampoo bottles (not too hard) we start laughing ha ha can't breathe we're so funny such good friends our fights are so silly. Think I care anyway so what she comes to my voice recitals but never says I'm good at anything never looks with amazement at my shining talent never apologizes to me about anything I always have to apologize first our constant argument You're so good at everything But people like you better and there we stagnate because we don't want to switch do we I don't Wanda says we both say we feel sorry for people who aren't us, people who aren't friends as good as we are but I am pretty sure that isn't what I think any more and I doubt she does either

§　§　§

"I want to be *different* from everybody else," I say to Ernie on the telephone. It is eleven o'clock at night, and I am sitting in the dark on the basement stairs, whispering. "I want to be striking, dramatic, amazing."

"Me too," says Ernie.

"And also, I want to be a writer."

"Yeah, and I want to be a rock star. Who cares what we want, though. We'll probably end up with kids and a house in the suburbs just like everybody else."

"Not everyone lives in the suburbs, Ernie."

"Well, you know what I mean."

"I guess."

§ § §

Wanda and I are walking around the reservoir at Cobb's Hill. We walk single file, so we can drag our left hands along the iron bars of the fence. Sometimes Wanda is in front, sometimes me. The light on the water is sorrowful, somehow. It is about six o'clock at night and it is March.

"Today at the dentist," says Wanda, "I read in *Cosmo*..."

"You were reading *Cosmopolitan*?"

"I was at the *dentist!*"

"Okay, okay."

"...that in every couple one person loves the other person more. Isn't that horrifying? I mean that it can never, never be equal."

"A depressing thought if ever there was one."

"Anyhow so it was saying that you can divide the world up into people who'd rather love more and who'd rather love less, and I was thinking that obviously you and I would rather love less..."

"You mean more," I correct her; she misspoke, she meant to say more, of course.

"No, I mean less – I mean, wouldn't you prefer to love less?" Wanda looks over her shoulder at me. We have stopped walking, our hands gripping the ornate iron bars, our bodies leaning back in straight diagonal lines. "You want the *other* person to love more – it's safer that way! You're saying you wouldn't want that?"

"Well, no...I think if I wasn't the one who loved more, I don't think I'd bother loving the person at all because it would be like, like, like not worth the effort, you know?"

For a good five seconds after that neither of us says a word.

Finally I ask, exasperated, "So did you have any cavities?"

We notice this moment with interest, as it is a major philosophical discussion in which we do not agree. We don't talk about it again.

§   §   §

In seventh grade, soon after moving to Brighton, I sat next to Josh in Mrs. Pilchard-Bentley's Language Arts class mods 4-6. One day when he was out with the flu, I penciled on his desk in a big heart **IDT INDT Josh Loves Dora.** For one week I arrived expectantly into Mrs. Pilchard-Bentley's class prepared for Josh to ask me out, or at least sit with me at lunch or say "I really like you Dora, I think you are neat."

But Josh's flu went on and on and the school janitor cleaned the desks every night and I had to write it over again each morning. **IDT INDT Josh Loves Dora** in a heart. The janitor wiping off the desk did not nullify the statement of love, because I had thrown in the official safety measure initials: IDT INDT, If Destroyed True, If Not Destroyed True. Of course I had written the statement part backwards – I loved Josh, but wrote that he loved me – I inverted the order to work some kind of a spell and convince him. Seventh grade boys were quite malleable, I believed.

When Josh returned to school (pale and wan from days of french toast and *Bewitched*), he sat down at his desk in Mrs. Pilchard-Bentley's class and dropped his three-ring notebook right on top of the heart and didn't even notice it. He was totally oblivious. I was in despair.

Strangely, though, that very afternoon five minutes after the bell rang Josh happened to be at the corner of Monroe and Elmwood where I normally went straight, but could turn left. Josh was going left. I went left that day. Josh gallantly inquired whether or not I had ever played a particular video game. I had not; I only had an old Atari.

What a romantic two hours we spent, jumping video smurfs over video mushrooms! How happy I was! Josh said he even would have invited me to his bar mitzvah earlier that year if he had known my last name.

For three weeks we were a couple. This meant we walked together after school to the arcade or (on one exciting occasion) went to Sharkey's on the weekend to roller skate. We did not sit with each other at lunch or ever touch, but I gained a certain status among the seventh grade girls for having a boyfriend, and Josh got punched in the shoulder by his friend Simon. After three weeks, however, we stopped walking together. This meant we broke up.

§   §   §

Happ y in High School

wh o is happy in high school? mnake a list
startign here:

§ § §

People are reciting poetry in Wanda's living room. It is the Sunday before Spring Break and everyone can sleep late the next day, so this Galaxy meeting has turned into a party.

Wanda begins the recitations with Robert Frost ("Something there is which does not love a wall...") and Monica chimes in with some Ferlinghetti. Norris, back from France and ultra-sophisticated in his new turtleneck, recites about ten pages from the *Canterbury Tales* in old English, causing many Galaxy members to adjourn to the kitchen in search of snacks. Wanda is deliberately ignoring him because she found out he cheated on her while he was in France; she has no intention of ever speaking to him, ever ever again. Her fury is carefully focused: she has told me she will wait until he crawls on his hands and knees, begging her forgiveness, but she will not take him back.

Simon does a Richard Brautigan; Yvonne Pie surprises everyone by knowing a Margaret Atwood poem ("You fit into me like a hook into an eye / a fish hook / an open eye") and Ray does a Gwendolyn Brooks. Josh recites a love poem and won't tell who wrote it ("Someone very obscure," he says).

I feel one inch tall: I do not know any poems by heart. I am dumb. I can only think of single lines ("Petals on a wet black bough") ("Love is not all, it is not meat nor drink") ("Die, and find death good") ("Nooses give. You might as well live.") ("And when you turned in your sleep, I turned with you"). I resolve to go home and start memorizing as soon as the party is over.

After a while the poetry drips out of everyone, and we play Wanna Buy a Duck, then Sardines, then I Love You Baby But I Just Can't Smile, then Murder In the Dark.

I walk across the street to my house at two in the morning, trying to remember the rest of the Edna St. Vincent Millay sonnet. Love is not all...Nor fire nor a something something rain, nor yet blah blah blah blah and rise and sink and rise and sink again. It well may be! I do not think I would!

§   §   §

From the margin of my English notebook:

I am showered in mythological heroes,
the earth mother archetype, dying
and reviving gods. But all I can think of
is Ernie, waiting at my locker
when I leave. He takes me in his mother's car
to McDonald's where we will share
twenty chicken mcnuggets with extra
sweet and sour sauce. Sex with him
is tangy like a grapefruit with sugar
you eat with a spoon that has spikes.
My english teacher makes us do
creative projects but I study on Sunday nights
in Ernie's bedroom, and learn only by accident
about the fall and the garden.
Ernie and I are falling, falling

like the Wizard of Oz witch melts

§   §   §

"It's really great not having a boyfriend, you know?" Wanda says to me, as if we're in the middle of a conversation, when actually we're just beginning one.

"It is?" I say, not sure where this is going.

"Yeah," says Wanda, idly, as though it's totally obvious to everyone. "Now that I don't have Norris hanging around me, I have time to do all kinds of things. I mean, it's amazing how much time I wasted on that guy. I'm glad I got rid of him."

I hadn't realized that Wanda had been in charge of that situation. I agree, tentatively, that it must be nice to have more free time, but I don't quite know what to say next. I have no intention of breaking up with Ernie just so she and I can be the same.

"Yes, I think I'm going to stay single for a long time," Wanda continues. "I don't need a boyfriend to make me happy."

§   §   §

While Josh comments on #82 at Galaxy meeting, Wanda stares at him inordinately. She has a strange look in her eye. It's not *that* difficult of a poem to understand – obviously a poem to someone the author looks up to, admires. Is something going on here? Is it a love poem?

"I think the 'intimidating forest' stands for, you

know, society, and it's a 'path of infinite length' because there's, like, no escape..."

Wanda is nodding as though she and Josh have a special understanding. I am totally left out. I wonder if they have been having secret conversations, because Wanda will not answer my questions about Josh, deflecting them with a joke or another question; apparently, she has something to hide and just doesn't want to discuss the issue even with her supposed best friend in the universe. It seems obvious that I am involved in some way, that the poem may be about me. I will have to prepare some way of letting Josh down easy.

§   §   §

Thoughts on The Breakfsast Club

great movie!
Finally, a movie in which teengangers transcend stereotypes and try to get to knwo each other as human being s.
transcend my ass! there es no MOlly RInglawd in thes school. There es no straeght-out-basket case with dandruff to make pectures.
I agree. Teh movie totally oversimplified our lives!
But waht else could it do? It only had a 2 hours (and a bitchin soundtrack) so it couldn't tell everyone's story.
It didnt' tell my story

it dind't tell mystory

Still, I think it is the defining flim of our generation.

that's really drepserespping. I mean depressing.

I think it's really drepserespping too. And also depressing.

You mean I have have to learn that funny dance step to be in my own generation?

that movie was made by adults who think they understand us.

But emilio esteves is my honey

no he is my honey

I didn't even see the movie yet so every one shut uyyp! shut up!

what pisseed me off is taht 'Nerd' character was such a 'Nerd' character he was not a real character. He did not do anythign but be a ner dthe whole movie.

Yeah, where were we in that movie? cool nersds

go write your own movie then

§   §   §

"Where's Wanda?"

"She's in class, dope. You know she has AP History mods 4-6."

"Okay, good, um, Dora, you know that poem at the last Galaxy meeting?"

"Yeah, that nice love poem, 'in dreams when you ask me' or something, what about it?"

"Well, uh, I, uh, did you like it?"

"Yeah, I thought it was great! Who wrote it, anyway?"

"Well that's the thing. I did."

"You wrote it! You wrote a mushy love poem! Wow!"

"..."

"Why are you telling me this?"

"Well, uh, I wanted to talk to you about this, because it's kind of important, well actually it's very important."

"Oh, Josh, what are you saying? Are you saying what I think you're saying?"

"I guess you've figured it out by now."

"I did suspect, but..."

"So what do you think she'd do, if I, you know, told her?"

"What would... Oh, what would Wanda do? Well, what would she do. You know what? I don't know."

"Could you find out for me?"

"No I could not find out for you! Find out for yourself! Am I supposed to do everything? I'm sorry, I'm sorry, let me think about this, are you sure you want to do something about this, are you sure it's not just some kind of temporary insanity?"

"I wish it were."

§   §   §

From my journal:

wrong, wrong, wrong. boy was I wrong. I was wrong about almost everything! I feel very stupid. I think it is probably the worst feeling in the world, to find out that someone has been hiding something from you. At least no one ever sees what I write in here, not even Wanda. Not that I <u>mind</u>, I mean it doesn't make any difference, it's not like I had decided for sure about anything, I just thought oh phone's ringing gotta go

§   §   §

After play rehearsal, Josh drives me home. Then he goes over to Wanda's house to proclaim his love. I wish him all the luck in the world. I have no idea what Wanda will say. That is a new feeling, not to know what Wanda thinks about something.

His car is still there an hour later. How do I know that? Because I can see it from my bedroom window, if I get up close and look from one side. On the way home we sang through the whole show together. We know all the songs by heart after so many times through.

Ten o'clock is when I normally call Ernie, but it's after ten now and I'm still sitting here. I wonder if I should take the phone off the hook so I'm not interrupted in my car-watching vigil. Which makes no sense, I know, but here I am still doing it.

"Okay, Galaxians, on to the next. Poem #88, 'Tanglewood.' Before we begin our discussion, let me just say that Dora and I think this is probably the best poem to come along all year."

"Hey, I thought we weren't supposed to talk about the value of the poem!"

"You know, this reminds me of something."

"Yes, Gina? What does the poem evoke for you? That's what really matters, and although it is true that Wanda and I love this poem, that doesn't mean everyone has to have the same reaction."

"It definitely reminds me of something...I can't put a name on it. What is it? Oh, yeah! This reminds me of camp. Waking up so early, and the smell, and the people. This reminds me of camp, and I hated camp! I *hated* camp! I hated the people! I hated waking up and that smell. And I hate this poem!"

"Oh brother."

§   §   §

It is pouring rain and everything is canceled. The rain will turn to ice and the school wants everybody to leave, to fall and slip outside the official boundaries.

The Wandora Unit rushes home under a single umbrella, miserable, not wanting to share. "Ugh Ugh Ugh" we cry in a single voice until reaching Wanda's house, where we happily separate onto the benches in the kitchen nook to be amazed as everything freezes.

Outside, the trees become wind chimes, each branch, each bud encased in ice. It is like another world. The light looks fake.

And in one hour it all drips away and it is actually spring and we have to go back to school the next day.

§   §   §

```
YAH Glorious spreeeeeeeeeeng!
     no more pencils
     nomore books
     no mroe teachers
     dirty looks
     crummy schnooks
     rotten crooks
     didn't I tell you people not to rhyme in
here?
     Norris drinks Livoris
     what's livoris
     I don't know but it sounds nasty


school is almost over hurray
```

§   §   §

"I don't know about you, but I feel reeeeeeally goooooood right now," says Ernie, who has adapted a sort of jazz drawl for post-fooling-around talk.

"Hmmmmmm," I sing in a smiling hum.

We are not too young to be having sex. We *are* having sex, every chance we get. Sex is our after-school special. Once we even fooled around in the Galaxy room! Sex makes our pimples go away. Sex is as wonderful as it will ever be, because it is bad, bad in the sense of getting away with something; we have no privacy so we have to make a private universe.

While I lie with Ernie in his bed in his bedroom at four o'clock in the afternoon during the window of opportunity before his parents come home from work, I feel the weighty presence of our two brains, our two worlds with the bridge of sex between them.

"You put the *u* in unique," I say.

"You put the *nique* in unique," responds Ernie, who is falling asleep in the luxury of the remaining half hour. Soon I will have to get on my bike and ride home.

But not quite yet and the bed seems so big; the bed is a world too; an enormous world and Ernie's mother drives into the driveway and I am suddenly in all my clothes, my bra stuffed in my backpack, and Ernie and I are doing our math and we are completely innocent and Ernie's mother truly does not suspect a thing, because she does not want to see how sweaty we are, how happy.

Ernie's mother actually brings us a bowl full of gummy bears and wishes us luck on our final exams!

§ § §

"#93 reminds me of Frank O'Hara."
"I think it's supposed to – I think it's an homage."

"I think it's a ripoff."

"How come the names are changed? To protect the innocent?"

"No, to protect the anonymity of the poet. If the poem makes it into the magazine, we'll change the names back."

"I have another question. What the heck are 'tree ears'?"

"Exotic mushrooms, I think. This poem is too symbolic."

"Too symbolic? What are you talking about? It's too specific."

"I like that it's specific."

"I hate it."

"It's too personal. There's actual names in there!"

"I think," says Wanda, who seldom uses that phrase, "That friendships have to end. That the poem is saying that friendships end."

This happens to be exactly right, but Wanda is cheating. It is her name whited out and covered up with another name.

§   §   §

```
the NOWHERE BOY saga continues

one day Nnowhere Boy came to the school.
He was new. He did not know how to play any of
the school games.
what is this crazy kickball? he asked. You
```

have to run to first base, like this, said
Timothy Toomothy, And then you ahve to jump
this rope. Thenyou have to pick up this pin
with your fett.

'With my fett? I think you mean feet' said
nowhere boy. Okay, ssaid Timothy Toomeothy,
Its just that I have this porblem. I speak in
typos.

nowhere boy went to lunch in the cafeteria.

'I wiill have an order of of french fries, a
chocolate milck, a donut, a bag of zues chips,
and a nutty buddy' said nowhere Boy. 'A La
Carte?' said the lunch lady.

'What?' said Nowhere Boy, not knowing what a
la carte was.

Then Nowhere boy went to the Galaxy room. What
are you doing? he said.

We are writing a story' said Zeena Zanana.

'Can I write in it too?' asked no whwere boy.

'Sure, it's your turn' said Drusila
Smepmampapki.

'My turn,' said nowhere boy. 'I wonder what I
will write.'

§   §   §

On the opening night of the play, I suddenly realize
that I far prefer rehearsal to performance. Acting without
an audience is satisfying; acting with people watching just
makes me anxious. I feel dishonest – much as I may relate

to the character I am playing, I am not Dolly Levi. I want to apologize as I say my lines, say to the audience, "This isn't really me."

I get a lot of flowers before and after the play, including a big bunch of lilies from Wanda. Most of the flowers are from people I barely even know. It makes me feel totally weird.

From Josh, Simon, and Ray, of course, I receive no flowers. That's not their style. They chip in and buy me a big piece of wood. "We wanted to get you something really heavy," they say. "Flowers are boring." It is the one gift I really like.

After the play everyone packs into the hallway next to the auditorium, hugging, yelling congratulations, saying "You were wonderful." I don't believe a word of it. The play is not really very good at all, but it's nice of people to say so. All this affection from strangers, however, is meaningless. Wanda assumes that I enjoy the attention, that I love having everyone in the school know who I am for a while. But it doesn't make me feel good. I'd actually rather not have it. It's messing things up.

§   §   §

I am crying in my bedroom for some reason unknown even to myself, which makes me cry all the more. I do it quietly, so no one in the house can hear, and when I am through, I stand in front of the mirror, say to myself, "This is what I look like when I've been crying."

It is not a pretty sight. My face is all blotchy and I

have snot above my lip. I am disappointed; I hoped I would look romantic. "I must never cry in front of anyone," I tell myself. "This is just not attractive."

§ § §

"Comments on #97, 'Ode to School'?"

"Dr. Seuss, but depressed."

"Makes me think of that poem by, um, whatsername, that one that says at the end "The joke is all over us.""

"I think that's Charles Bukowski."

"I think it's Gwendolyn Brooks."

"I don't even know what you are talking about."

"According to this poem, school is a dream."

"One you have no power over."

"I like the e.e. cummings-esque small i's."

"Dora and I do not. In fact, didn't we make a rule about that?"

"You can't make rules about other people's poetry!"

"But we can make rules about what goes into Galaxy. Right Dora?"

"Yes, that's right, but..."

"I think that in this case the small i's are good. The speaker in the poem obviously feels very small and insignificant."

"But small i's call attention to themselves, by virtue of their smallness!"

"Still, I think they make sense here."

"Yvonne, you're awfully quiet, do you have an

opinion on this matter?"

"Um, no."

"But you always have an opinion!"

"Wanda, leave her alone."

"Yeah, let's go on to the next poem, okay? This one seems pretty straightforward."

§   §   §

Wanda and I return from the printer's full of information and excitement. Galaxy is almost done for the year.

"So these are the wingdings? These wavy lines around the page numbers?"

"Yeah. Are we going to have those? I like that font called Zapf."

"I like the name more than the font itself."

"Me too."

"I wish there were different fonts for different voices – like a font for the Martian on Bugs Bunny."

"The guy who says 'I will exterminate you' and tries to blow up the earth?"

"Yeah, him."

"Yeah, and a font for the duh voice."

"Yeah, a stupid font, and a sarcastic font."

"How would the sarcastic font look?"

"I picture it kind of sideways, not tilted but turned."

"There should be a special font for each emotion – one for anger, one for hunger, one for love, one for giggliness, one for anxiety, one for lust."

"Is lust an emotion?"

"Is hunger?"

§   §   §

Before Galaxy meeting, late on a Sunday afternoon, Wanda and I walk up to Cobb's Hill to run around the reservoir. Wanda is faster so she will go around once and then turn back and run the other way until she meets me, and then we will walk home together in time to get to Galaxy meeting at Ray's.

It is five o'clock already and it will get dark at six. Soon Wanda is out of my sight. I do not have a good attitude about exercise; I can only think about how tired I am, how much I dislike running and how badly my knees hurt. The reservoir seems huge when you have to run all the way around it.

The water reflects the sun in postcard style glory, but I remember when they drained the reservoir once and found guns, broken bicycles, a dead cat and an entire car. I wonder what is in there now.

When the street lamps go on I am pretty sure I am on my second lap, but I have not seen Wanda. I start to get a little nervous. There is no one else around.

I stop running, gaze through the iron bars across the water, do not find Wanda anywhere. I climb up on a bench, wondering if perhaps Wanda has stopped and is looking for *me*. I start yelling Wanda's name at the top of my voice. Panic rises in me like a bad poem. I walk back and forth along one curve of the path as it gets darker and darker and the lights in the city start to go on. Wanda is not answering. She is not there.

We are circling and circling, somehow missing each other with each step. I might stay here forever, waiting uselessly in the cold and danger rather than abandon my best friend, but Wanda takes action: she runs back to our street in a burst of fearful endorphins, finds my mother at home, and gets her to drive them both back to Cobb's Hill, where they find me almost in tears.

"Where *were* you?"

"Where were *you*?"

"I was so worried!"

"I don't understand it!"

"Didn't you hear me yelling? I have the loudest voice in the world!"

"I didn't hear a thing."

"Next time, let's not separate."

"Next time, let's not come here at all. It's too easy to lose someone."

It is the only time we miss a Galaxy meeting. Without the Wandora Unit, believe it or not, the meeting goes just fine.

§   §   §

"#107 rhymes, but it knows it rhymes."

"It's hilarious!"

"It's stupid."

"What's it about?"

"Vomiting in someone's car..."

"Love..."

"Turtles..."

§   §   §

After the final voting meeting the following week, Wanda and I stay up all night putting the finishing touches on the magazine. By two in the morning, cramped into the Galaxy room, we begin to argue.

"What do you *mean* we don't have room for Gina's light switch poem?" I ask. "All we have is room! Remember, we asked for lots of white space?"

"Gina's poem is simply not up to the standards of the rest of the magazine. Just because people voted for it doesn't force us to print it."

"On the other hand, not very many people voted for Josh's poem, the one about amber whatever, but we're printing that."

"Josh's poem is well-written. We print things that are well-written."

"Well, I mean of course I think it's good too, but it's hard to be objective, since it's about you, and everything."

"Is that what's bothering you?"

"I think it's terrific that he wrote a poem about you! Of course I do! He's my friend too, and I think he's a great writer! I just mean, objectively speaking, that poem didn't get many votes, and neither did the other one, the "in dreams when I ask you" one. And I think some people might say that isn't fair."

"Are you implying that I'm not being fair?"

"No, no, I'm not saying that." I back off carefully. "I think we're capable of being objective, and that's why we ought to put aside our personal feelings for Gina and look at the poem. It's a decent poem, and I think it should go in. I think Josh's poems should go in too."

"Good, I'm glad we agree."

"We agree?"

Although I have won the fight over the inclusion of Gina's poem, I feel defeated. This issue of Galaxy has defeated me, and Wanda has too. Our friendship no longer feels like two trees growing together and intertwining; instead, I feel as though I am being bent to someone else's will. And talking to Wanda is sometimes like talking to a stranger on a bus, a stranger you wish would leave you alone.

It pains me to suspect that Wanda is experiencing the same thing. I want to think that I am the only one who notices that our conversations have become stupid, so that we don't even want to talk to each other anymore, but this is not so. I think she must see it too. It's not that we dislike each other – not yet, anyway. We just aren't thinking and acting as the Wandora Unit anymore.

§   §   §

When I was five years old, I sat on the landing of the staircase in my grandmother's house in Wellsville. The carpet was a gaudy spring green, the color of green food coloring or Easter egg dye.

I was completely alone there, except for my favorite toy, an enormous six foot long furry snake with a red felt tongue. I wrapped the snake around the banister and played on the landing while the grown-ups made dinner and put 1000-piece puzzles together and played Scrabble.

Occasionally a grown-up went up or down the stairs and paused to talk to me, but I was very busy. I was polite to the grown-ups but really I was in a bright green world with my snake. The fibers of the rug made a weird pastel forest where my snake and I walked. The snake walked. The forest was full of creeks and pools and living things. It was like a movie and the snake and I were the only characters.

§   §   §

At the Galaxy publication party, a whole bunch of us – me and Wanda and Simon and Ray and Bill Brunheuber and Yvonne Pie and the habitually depressed Carl Jacobs – have crushed ourelves into the wardrobe in Wanda's parents' bedroom and are trying not to laugh.

We are playing sardines – a reversed form of hide and seek in which whoever is "It" hides and the rest seek. When you find the hiding person you have to hide *with* him or her until everyone is hiding, and the last person to try to get into the hiding place has to hide the next time.

Inside of the wardrobe it is very hot and it is getting obscene. I am not sure whose knee is pressed against my side, or whose arm is around me. All of Galaxy is becoming one big organic globule, its sum sweatier, smellier, lovelier than its parts.

Later, on the lawn, Ernie does his drool trick to keep the partygoers enthralled.

Galaxy is finished, and the Wandora Unit jointly cuts the red ribbon tied around a stack of magazines. There they are. They are splendid.

§ § §

From my journal:

Ernie's hands are...so warm against me I want to...curl up inside him like a snail I want to...get all over him, envelop him like a monstrous cloud...his lips are...the skin of him...his face...I go there after Galaxy meetings on Sunday nights...at Ernie's house we are studying...we study each other's bodies; we love each other...we make out for an hour and then do homework...Ernie kisses me everywhere...I want to, I don't know...Ernie's door does not lock...for months and months it is this way...sometimes I leave with my bra in my knapsack...flushed, happy, Ernie calls me "juicy," I touch his face with the back part of my fingers...kiss his eyelids...kiss him upside-down...he looks at me as though we are both about to die...we don't care... every Galaxy meeting is a prelude to this...we giggle, we cry, we tip over onto the floor...

§ § §

"...you *WHAT?*" I can hardly take it: Ernie is the ringleader, the main link in the chain of physics cheating? I become quieter than I have ever been, quieter than a sleeping four-year-old; my breathing can barely be heard. Because I am not breathing.

Did everyone know? Obviously Kevin Sullivan knew, he was helping, and that's why he and Ernie always quit talking as I arrived at Ernie's locker. I probably witnessed half of the transactions without realizing it! Did all my friends know, and not tell me? Josh must have known. Did Wanda know? I have been a total fool all along and they all knew it and they were all laughing at me and thinking I was a fool, which I was. Can there be anything good about this at all? This is INSANE! How could I not have noticed?

I am filling myself up with a massive tower of indifference, so that I can say goodbye to him. Because I know it is true, what I overheard accidentally in the hall, that Ernie is the one who has been stealing the physics exams from the teacher's office, photocopying them, and selling them to other students. That I have been in love with an asshole all this time – and I could have sworn it was Wanda who had chosen the loser, Norris. No, the prize is mine, I am going out with a boy who lies.

§   §   §

"Why did you do it?"

"It's not a big deal, Dora. You don't have to make such a huge thing out of it."

"It is a big deal. And you're not answering my question."

"What do you want me to say?"

"Anything but that."

§ § §

For three days, I do not say a word to anyone. I did not know it was possible, but I am able not to talk at all. My face trapped in a frown, I avoid my friends. Leave little notes so as not to arouse suspicion:

Mom: gone to voice lesson. Got ride with Josh. Home later.

Josh: don't need ride - taking the bus. Thanks anyway.

Mr. Coleman: sorry, can't make my lesson today. See you next week.

Wanda: had to get to school early for a meeting. Sorry.

I spend the afternoon under the jungle gym at the playground, journal in hand, not writing anything. Everything has been ending for so long anyway. I just want everything to be over.

The next day in English class, I do not have anything to add to the discussion of *Lord Jim*. I do not raise my hand once. Ms. Green is surprised, asks, "Dora, don't you have anything to say on this subject?" A quick shake of the head. No, I don't. I have no opinion on Joseph Conrad. I have no opinion on anything.

The three days go by and no one notices my silence. I was making about ten percent of the total noise in school, but apparently it was all unnecessary noise. No one misses it. No one asks me what is wrong. Not even Wanda, who seems to be avoiding me. I am ready at all times with an answer ("Don't mind me – I'm just tired") but she doesn't ask. Nothing is wrong, anyway. Nothing at all.

I am casting about for something to keep me from slipping away completely – sweeping in concentric circles outside myself – and coming up with nothing solid.

How could he not *tell* me? I assumed he told me everything. I thought that was the definition of love, that you had no secrets from each other. If he had let me in on it from the beginning, I might (stranger things have happened) willingly have gone along with it, become his sly and conniving partner in petty crime, acting as lookout or as copygirl. Wanda and I have never done much rule-breaking; we have always preferred *making* the rules; sex has always been my great transgression, and it has always been enough for me.

I try to come up with some reason why what Ernie did is okay. Like: the teachers are stupid not to notice and it's their responsibility. Or: it's just like the real world; in the real world people cheat all the time and get away with it and become huge successes.

But the problem isn't that Ernie did something immoral or stupid, it's that he could do it behind my back. He kept it a secret all this time, all those hot Sunday nights, all those private cuddles in the Galaxy room, I wouldn't have told. I have a big mouth but I think I could have kept it closed if I needed to. Really, I could have. Probably.

Now there is no love, or only a buried love, and I have to keep quiet anyway, which just totally sucks, and the only thing to do is keep to myself, because my loyalties are suddenly all up in the air. Not telling Wanda is the hardest thing, and I can only avoid spilling the truth to my best friend by avoiding the friendship completely.

§   §   §

We sit, typewriter in hand,
Pulling loneliness around us

– Nikki Giovanni, "Poetry"

§   §   §

The first time Ernie ever told me he loved me it was because I said I loved him. I said, "So what if I love you? Is that so terrible? What are you going to do, run out of the Galaxy room screaming?"

It was mod 17 on day four, in January. We were about to go home. Ernie said, "I guess if you love me, I have no choice but to love you back. I do love you back. And I love your back."

"And I love your backpack."

"And I love your snackpack."

We left the building, and the sky was gray, but we

were pink. It was about to snow. I walked Ernie to his bus and he kissed me goodbye in front of everyone.

But what did he do when he got home? Did he call Kevin up and make plans for the disbursement of tests the next day? I don't even know the correct terminology for this shit. Is every memory of my time with Ernie ruined? Now everything with Ernie has a dark, shadowy quality; I can't trust myself on that subject. I know in the past I would have run to Wanda to talk about it, but my friendship with Wanda now seems pinched and unreal. I am glad I haven't been talking to Wanda, because I would get no sympathy there, anyway, just a kind of gloating: Wanda would be pleased that Ernie hurt me. What he has done is even worse than Norris's affair; she would make it into a binding act: now the Wandora Unit has been scorned by its ex-boyfriends and should wreak revenge.

§   §   §

```
I hasd this dream of the library and there were
all these fat women! WHy did I dreamthis?
I don't know and I don't care about youur
fat women. I had a dream of my own about the
library. I dreamed the lbiary went on and on
and the book I wanted kept moving and I was
annoyed but then the book led me to all these
other books! In a big red room with carpet on
the books all the books I ever wanted to read!
Also I could read with my eyes closed
The only dream I ever had about the library
```

was I dreamed the library lady Mrs. Finkle had
fangs.
Mrs. Finkle really does have fangs.
I dreamed I ate a full course meal in the
library and Mrp. Finlke told me I was banished
from teh library forever and I started to cry!
Right inthe lirbary! As if i care if I could
never go back to the library.
I dreamed I was in the library and I was, well,
I was, well, it's alittle embarrassing to say,
but I was........masturbating.
I dream that all th e time!
me too!
your all a bunch of perversts I never go in the
libray and now I'm definitley not.
I never have any dreams

§   §   §

On the fourth day I return to the world of the
speaking, but only nominally. When the lunch lady asks if
I want my french fries a la carte, I could just nod my head,
but instead I answer yes. And "yes" I say, yes I would, yes.
And I start to cry.

The lunch lady gives me a blank stare. "They're
only french fries, honey."

"Thank you," I say. Sprinkle the salt.

"What's the matter, honey? Boyfriend troubles?"

"No," I sniff, "I don't really care about that. That's
not the problem." I start eating the fries, holding up the

lunch line behind me. "It's nothing really. I just haven't talked to my best friend in a while, that's all."

"Well go talk to her! What are you waiting for?"

"No, see, I don't really want to. I don't want to talk to her."

"You know, I know what you mean. Next? a la carte?"

§   §   §

I dream I am reading a novel that seems strangely familiar. The author is Wanda, but she has stolen all the good lines from me. The pages are filled with my words! The photograph on the back even looks like me! In the dream, Wanda does not understand why I am angry. "We're the same," she says, "we don't have any secrets. Why shouldn't we write the same book?"

When I wake up, I am relieved to be in my own room, my favorite sweatshirt hanging from the doorknob, poetry journal on the desk. I resist the urge to check the journal to make sure my words are intact. Wanda cannot do me any harm. I stay in bed until I am absolutely sure of this, and then get up for school.

§   §   §

"But why are you making such a big deal out of it?" Ernie cannot fathom why I am still angry. He figured I would come around. Instead I am suddenly even farther away. I won't even look at him.

"Because you lied."

"I never lied. I never said anything that was a lie." Ernie's voice is cracking. He can't believe this is happening. He thought he and I would be together forever.

"Not telling me is a lie. It's the same thing. But it doesn't matter. I just don't love you anymore," I say. We are outside the Galaxy room after school, empty halls in all directions. Only the distant sound of the track team running stairs reaches us. By saying it out loud, I have made it true. I want Ernie to go away before I change my mind.

"Yeah, well..." says Ernie, not realizing that he could talk me out of it. "Whatever," he sobs out, and takes off.

§   §   §

Wanda and I were trying on hats in After Eden on Monroe Avenue. Hat after hat, at five dollars each.

"Do you like this one?" I set a red beret rakishly. It was October, and we were all psyched up to attend the homecoming dance.

"In this one I look like Mrs. Finkle."

"Here, try on this – it has a veil."

"Do you think the guy who owns this place realizes we have no intention of buying anything?"

"Speak for yourself – I think I need this blue flowered thing."

"That looks like a bathing cap."

"That's why I like it."

§   §   §

"Could you believe it, our maid just got up and quit yesterday, without a bit of notice."

"No!"

"Yes! I'm at my wit's end – I mean what am I supposed to do? I'm at the club all day until three – I can't just run home and take care of the kids and fix dinner and do everything!"

"No, no, of course you can't."

"Other people manage it," said Wanda, stuck in the line with me at Wegmans behind these two ladies, who had twenty-two and eighteen items, respectively, in the ten items or less aisle.

"How rude!" exclaimed the lady with twenty-two items.

"But how right," I chimed in. We were trying not to laugh. These ladies were buying squeeze-margarine and maxi-pads. They were buying frozen corn on the cob in the middle of July.

The ladies went on their way, immediately ignoring the Wandora Unit. The Wandora Unit was beneath their contempt. These ladies forgot about the Wandora Unit as soon as they picked up their two bags of groceries from the conveyor belt and got in their cars. But Wanda and I were filled with mirth over and past the moment, until we were struck with fear: will we become like these ladies?

"No," said Wanda. "We will never be like them, because we would never, never take more than ten items into the ten items or less lane."

§ § §

It was 7:08 in the morning and Wanda and I were marching down the main hall of the school in our winter coats. Ernie, who had not yet fallen in love with me and barely knew me, stood at his locker watching us pass, and for the second that he bothered to think about it he hated us, those two girls in the long coats who obviously thought they were queens of the world.

§ § §

I have started picking my fingernails again. I'm brutal. The cuticles of my right hand are bleeding, and the nails look gnawed. I haven't done this since I was twelve.

I try to separate my hands but they keep coming together, picking, picking, my hands will never look nice, I will never have hands as nice as Wanda's, as smooth, feminine, pretty.

§ § §

The grass so little has to do
I wish I were a hay

– Emily Dickinson

This is the Galaxy door saying good luck on finals everybody!

§ § §

Something has been happening all along. At the same time that all this is going on – Galaxy meetings, play rehearsals, Model U.N. meetings, track meets, classes, report cards, romances, eating, sleeping, and going to the bathroom – at the same time, something else has been happening. Like when you are reading along in a book and suddenly you realize that for the past two and a half pages you have been worrying about your job or planning the order in which you'll do your errands.

Wanda and I have been separating ourselves. We are breaking apart like a dangerous iceberg in the middle of the Antarctic Sea. "Thank God, Cap'n, I think she's breaking apart!" "Tell the crew not to begin celebrations until we're certain."

No single event causes it, but by the time school ends, we are strangers. The Wandora Unit shatters in a million pieces spreading outward in the expanding universe.

§ § §

"Where's Wanda?"
"How should I know?"

§ § §

I go to the senior prom with Bill Brunheuber. Wanda goes with Josh. Everyone is nervous and has a terrible time. The prom is supposed to be this incredible ending to everything, but really it's just a fizzle. The band doesn't play good music, and the girls get runs in their incredibly expensive stockings, and all the students get almost high on lack of sleep and giggling at everything, but it's all totally dumb. I don't think I've ever heard a grown-up talk about what a great time the prom was. If anything, they just compete for who had the worst time.

By the end of the evening Wanda and I are each horribly disappointed. We were supposed to go to this event together, a double date focusing on *us*. Instead we each find ourselves faced with an adoring, clueless boy who proclaims undying love without understanding anything.

§   §   §

"What's wrong?" asks Bill Brunheuber, turning bright red, embarrassed beyond belief that he just told me he could picture us married one day. His tuxedo fits him poorly.

"I'm sorry," I say, trying to figure out why in the world I am not having a good time at the prom.

"I shouldn't have said anything."

"No, no, don't let anything make you feel that way," I say, suddenly fiercely angry at myself. "I can picture it too. No, really, I can." And suddenly I do. I picture all kinds of things in the future. The prospect of going to college, growing up, perhaps getting married and having children or becoming a famous author or being a back-up singer in a punk band…all these things seem possible. The future looms up in front of me, and more than anything, I want to walk into it alone. I don't want to be one-half of a unit, one leg dragging another body my direction, Siamese twins pulling in opposite ways. *Alone* has begun to rhyme with *freedom*.

§ § §

At graduation, I sit next to my "husband," Matthew Nussbaum, because everything is in alphabetical order. He leans over me during the principal's speech and tells me that he has to take a piss really bad. He has been drinking all day with the football team, and his mortarboard is falling off his head. I pin his hat on correctly and tell him please to shut up.

The whole graduating class sits in the red velvet seats of the Eastman Theater, yearbooks, Galaxys, and programs in their laps. Most of the Galaxys will end up on the floor, forgotten, unread.

§ § §

The only thing I can say for sure is that we're all wrong. Every one of us. I don't think there's any specific *reason* for any of it – or if there is, I don't know it.

Does it bother me? Yes – but not in a tragic way. I mean, what difference would it make if I knew exactly *why* our friendship ended? We still wouldn't want to be best friends any more.

You know, the thing about all those girls in the books - Alice in Wonderland, Dorothy in Oz, Lucy in Narnia -

they all get to go to these other, magical worlds, but they never get to stay. What does that mean? I guess they can go back, in the sequels of course, but each time, they return to the real world. (Except Dorothy in one of those later Oz books, she gets to stay forever, but she never gets any older, she stays a kid forever, that's kind of like going crazy.)

I think it's like reading (or writing) a book – you get to go to this place for a while, but in the end you have to return to the regular world. The book ends, but you don't. You keep going, in a place where the reader can't see you.

§   §   §

I have a repeating dream, a dream I've had since I was very small. In it, I am holding someone's hand, and looking out over a tree-filled cliff. The colors are amazingly vivid, like when you turn the color knob on the TV too far to the right. My hold is very precarious. In the dream, I hang there a moment, and then let go of the hand.

Once, climbing the steep side of Cobb's Hill, I had a similar experience to this: Josh, Simon, and Wanda were around me, hanging on to thin tree trunks and scuffling upward toward the reservoir. The leaves were dry and slippery, and I slipped.

I made no sound, just slid fifteen feet or so down the steep slope until my foot caught in a hollow and I had time to grab on to a bunch of weeds, tough goldenrod that withstood my yanking. My friends barely noticed I was gone, until I let out a kind of yelp, and then they clamored down for me, their bodies moving confidently down the almost-cliff to help me stand up.

The strange thing is, I remember having the falling dream even before that day, all the way back to when I slept in a little bed and had one of those lamps that spin animals and shapes on the wall. Did the dream predict the future? Or did I make up this memory?

It could be that the dream is just symbolic, no more attached to the past or the future than any other moment.

Sometimes, after letting go of the hand in the dream, I fall slowly past all the trees, like Alice down the rabbit-hole in Wonderland. Other times there is a lag in the fall, so that time slows down until I wake up. And occasionally I don't seem to fall at all, just pause there, or if I fall, I'm falling upward – the trees extending away from me, the sky moving toward me.

Am I falling, or floating? Could it be that I am flying?

GALAXY

staff: Monica Braverman, Bill Brunheuber, Ray M. Clark, Simon Edwards, Judy Gage, Ernest Goldstein, Suzie Grass, Carl Jacobs, Melissa Klein, Talya Liebowitz, Gina Marcone, Yvonne Pie, Noris Robbins, Josh Shapiro.

GALAXY

GALAXY

The official literary magazine of Brighton High School
edited by Wanda Lowell and Dora Nussbaum

TABLE OF CONTENTS

A Poem

A poem is not for throwing. And never
ever yell. A poem must have rhyme;
a poem should not smell. A poem needs
a rhythm, count syllables with care.
A poem should have reason, a poem should
be fair. A poem is just like a judge
or lawbook or a king, a poem should
not break the jaw, a poem can't do
everything. A poem should not steal
or lie or get bad grades or fail,
a poem should set an example
and never go to jail. A poem should speak
only truth and never use sarcasm;
why anyone would want to write
a poem, I can't fathom.

– Monica Braverman

Ode to School

sometimes i sit
and often wonder
just what the hell
is going under
i am one
what can i do
makes no difference
when i'm through
i don't know why
but there is hate
however i try
it's still too late
i was never here
but now i'm gone
some feel the guilt
and write a song
when it's over
and they are free
who's going to rule
they can't agree
then it rains
and that's all through
how will they live
what can they do
i thought i was asleep
but then i woke
i forgot the line
what was the joke

                       – Yvonne Pie

Blueberries

He asked me if,
As he was my friend,
He could pick my blueberries,
If I minded him taking them away.
I don't mind, I said,
But they aren't my blueberries to say –
It's only my land that they're on.
They sprung up here once,
After the big fire
(Which I didn't plan)
They came like the birds that eat them,
Flying in one spring on the west wind.
The birds aren't mine
I let you listen when they sing
About the blueberries that live on my land.
When people come to pick these berries,
Not like you, not my friends,
We tell them
This is private property, get off – never
These are our blueberries.
Because they belong to whoever picks them.

     – Wanda Lowell

One Brief Moment

I step into the room
I flick the switch
For one brief moment
Darkness surrounds me
The light flickers
My imagination runs
Wild with terror
Luminescent light
Fills the room
I catch my breath
and enter

– Gina Marcone

the incompleteness, inconstancy of words.

    drunken
    sarcastim
    latin/laud inum
you are above me. we do not
use words, that fail
    hey now
    song, tongue
    filmature
    linguinium
and if there was a dictionary
(floating: above our heads)
to explain this language, could
we read it with our hands?
    your
    body
    not skin, mouth
    televi
    sion
    eyes or a bite of melon

– Bill Brunheuber

After School

this chair is tipping!
I'm trying to get a box
of Chinese tree ears out of the cupboard.
Hold on! We are making brownies!

Sometimes these brownies taste disgusting.
Wanda, why did you put peas in here?
You're jumping on the trampoline. It is
2:55 of a Thursday, right before school ends.
You look like you could fly off!

Let's go buy a pizza bagel at Murray's
to eat on the way home.
Simon is talking on a fake microphone
connected to a superlong cord
in the hallway at the highschool. He says
"put me in the poem!" But why?
"Because what I am doing is funny."
                    We are going
to college next autumn, so no more borrowing Josh's wristwatch.
But Wanda, where did you go? Inside the gymnasium
the kids are climbing up the poles
and you and I are wearing navy blue tights
we bought for $7 each 2 pair $12 at Archimage
before you go to New Hampshire
and take half of us away
                    – Dora Nussbaum

In dreams when I ask you
what kind of time we're having
and you answer something about yellowed grass
and trees with smooth, thin bark,
or maybe a blue sky
carrying guitar notes in a whipping wind,
perhaps what you are truly speaking of
is a day without a sunset, or
a night without a dawn,
where we provide the colors that
not even the marriage of night and day
could dream of.

– Josh Shapiro

Romance Novels

In those pretty monsters who came under the tables
where I sat eating apples and my brother cried
their flower slime was a comfort. Their falling voices
made my eyes pink. They threw me
away. In their jaws I was safe.

This lunging, these breaths. I hear their mewling
still. The sidewalk lurches upward, sucks me back.
Those things my mother used to read, the half-unbuttoned
blouses of women, the moustached men, the edges
of the page painted red or yellow, the carved out hole
with a face sticking through you always had to
look inside. Look there. Go there. Come

in those monsters. Those sidewinding wrecks.
Those jabberwocks, those mammoths, those precocious
brats with evil laughs could not come in
between the glass. I kept them out with my green hair.
I locked them away and saved them in a drawer.
I miss them. The loves of my life. Those books.

      – Karen Sung

A Walk on Monroe Avenue

reflections in the window
a woman, a baby

but it keeps on raining.

I think I'll go to McDonalds
I think I'll go to McDonalds

       – Ray M. Clark

No More to Abide in the Garden

There's a beauty in seeing reds and greens
when all there is white and black.
And there's a beauty in feeling someone's hand on your
shoulder
when you're alone in the room.
There too is a beauty in hearing laughter and singing
when it is only your mind imploding late at night.
In the silence (my voice)
In the darkness (my eyes)
In the void (my bloodied coat)
And then you realize that all your amazement,
all this spinning fantasy,
is the wicked fruit of a little white capsule,
and you are blind to the prism bloom,
seeing only a withered stem.

– Matthew Nussbaum

Tanglewood

How dense and dark
The forest looms
Amidst its shadows lie
The rhythms of its arms
enfold
Foreboding paradise

Gray luster flits
And beckons those
Who choose to fly astray
Beyond the beat-brush
Tanglewood
In liquid light of day

A sarcoid strain
of wind-wrapped boughs
Ply dusk into a gate
The cooling sigh of soil provides
A means to consecrate

How dense and deep
The forest lies
An island far away
The void engulfs, the sunlight burns
How far I cannot say
The hysteria of sunlight
How far I cannot say

– Rachel Anne Satter

Thank You

Thank you for coming,
Thank you for leaving.
Thank you for mumbling,
Thank you for screaming.
Thanks for the flowers,
Thanks for the dirt.
Thanks for the ashtray
And the turtle named Burt.
Thank you for the dinnerware,
Thanks for the lovely cup.
Thanks for the ride in your new car,
I'm sorry I threw up.

– Ray M. Clark

You went, and how long
it was before the ragged rhythm of crickets
in the brooding night got louder and fierce
as the trees sang dissonant lullabies, and I
lost your memory somewhere as I walked.
I was searching for you in the luminous flowers
who see tomorrow's promise in moonlight glow,
and I wanted to wait with them.

Left in this lush valley, the chasm of your absence,
almost blinded by thick night, I fended for myself
in the primeval forest.
I passed by a strange lake like melted sapphire
where pearly fish glided under glass and the sand was wet
gold.

I tried to go back to the flowers,
wanted to hear a familiar voice
in the song of the trees who knew you,
but I could not, and by and by
my eyes adjusted, catlike, to the night.

                    – Beth Wrubel

Jungle

You and I sit on your sofa in the jungle,
The note that makes the chord extraordinary is far away.
You dozily strum guitar,
Such is the pattern we easily fall into.
We have done this often before,
But I have been alone with myself since.
Evergreens and granite glacial streams and time
Overran the rhythm we lived to,
Installed in me their own.
The guitar plays louder in the jungle
So I look silently at the patterns bright sunshine makes on your
      textured wicker basket
Fading the drum of rain to the roar of cars in the jungle
So
the rhythm in my self is dulled
As the sunshine fades the basket's pattern to oblivion.

      – Wanda Lowell

School: A Start in Life?

I was living off the earth
on love, and happiness, just playing life's game.
Til one day it dawned upon me that
it was all a waste, losing time, losing face.
I began to work as never before.
The more I pondered, the more was piled upon me.

That dingy old building – a life institution
was eating me up, slowly, so slowly.
I couldn't last, at the rate I was going,
and that dingy old building kept eating and eating.
At last it reached my torn open heart,
the core of my life, the last light of hope,
and it swallowed that too, and now it's digesting me,
slowly, so slowly.

      – Carl Jacobs

Loom

We are two weavers of sticky tales
      that affix themselves in silken strangleholds
and it is the woven threads
      that, by chance it seems, bind two hearts into one.

Unbalancing act   confusion prevails
      he struggles with the sticky bit he weaves
that tangle up his thoughts
      until he discards them
but she sits silent
      as she often does
      smiling
      and observes as her love
unwinds the tales
that bind his mind.

And she touches him
and the spark of fingers
melts ice-cold edges.
They are against the
future,
watching sticky bits enflame
and the sky
      burns vermilion.

             – Suzie Grass

CLICK!

click!
I do not have time for television (monotone)
I do not have time for music (stereophone)
I am busy with the wonders of education!
(Of course this does lead to my deprivation
of fun.) But I am learning the beauty
of the written word, and the magic of
higher mathematics! (Where I practice my social tactics,
because school is where we learn to be cool.)
Science is a handy appliance, and with this construction
if you order now, comes extra my destruction
and therefore I do not have the time for you
nor do I have the time for me.
click!

(perhaps if I combined my parts
I could make use of the higher arts)

– Judy Gage

I see you, dressed in amber
The silhouette is a beautiful blend
Against the intimidating forest.

I don't know if I can impress you,
For you and your world may not accept me.
As we drift through black corridors,
You lend a trusting hand.
Your approving grip allows me to enter your world.

It will take several years for me to repay you.
The night that follows us will act as a guide
Through the path of infinite length.

The darkness that awaits us will contain
A sound of a limited world, filled with
Glowing shades of splendor.

This world is nothing compared to your limitless palace.
Yet its importance cannot be neglected.

For this world is only the start.
It is the first land which I have conquered with you
By my side.

                            – Josh Shapiro

Out onto the morning damp green
Bare feet found dew
Something forgotten
Smell of hot air
stings sleepburning eyes.
Pine trees cast white shadows
End in glaring pinpoint of blue light
in which Time has expanded,
Metamorphosed.
Voices cry an urgent plea
The ear hears only silence
for the crickets have ceased.
The oddity amazes.
A burst of darkness almost blinds,
Stillness overwhelms.
A mental hand reaches out in friendship
Bonding sleepdrugged mind
subconscious reigning over conscious thought.
An unexpected whir
The sight of mortal hand slapping alarm
Quiet.
White ceiling, focused visions recollected.
Strange dream.
But the first step has been taken –
The odyssey has begun.

– Melissa Klein

Cheshire Poem

this poem appears slowly, smile first
      do you know that its WHISKERS are better than its EYES
this poem talks to you out of a tree
      (poems can't talk but this seems perfectly normal)
there are huge red roses.

now it is all here. the rabbit's running away.
this poem can tell you the right path
      (like a certain scarecrow) but you
have to read the code.
don't let that rabbit go.

this poems disappears as mysteriously
      as it came to you. you can't be sure
when you will see it again, or
      what form it will take.
it might be a baby pig. it might be a dream.

– Dora Nussbaum

To Jar

Even with both hands spread
the shadows hold our tongue
It is sake they keep from us
though more than our own

You will believe this Sunday
when the plateau between soul and skin
shows its seams

the joke is all over us

Remember keep such words from air;
you have heard how words die: Once said
they resort to inhale, choking on their last letters
until only gasp abides

Such secrets in this jar
to be slid on the upper shelf
You can barely see the cotton nest
beneath the lid

– Bill Brunheuber

"It's beautiful," says Dora.

"It is the most beautiful thing we have ever done," says Wanda.

THE END

LaVergne, TN USA
26 November 2009
165357LV00001B/5/P